M. Night Shyamalan's

THE SIXTH SENSE

A novelization

M. Night Shyamalan's

THE SIXTH SENSE

A novelization

SCHOLASTIC INC.
New York Toronto London Auckland Sydney
Mexico City New Delhi Hong Kong

For Asher Kahn

ISBN 0-439-20163-2

12 11 10 9 8 7 6 5 4 3 2 1 0 1 2 3 4 5 6/0

Printed in the U.S.A.

First Scholastic printing, March 2000

PROLOGUE

On the night his life changed forever, Cole Sear was fast asleep. The air carried through his window the feel of a city in autumn — rain-soaked leaves, burning fireplaces, and car exhaust. Tonight, for a change, sleep had come easily. A little too easily. Down the hallway and just past the living room, his mother lay half awake, one ear cocked toward Cole's room. One scream, one gasp, one thump of a bare foot on the floor would send her running. For Lynn Sear, this night was the same as all others. She was worried about money, about her jobs, about her divorce, and always — *always* — about Cole.

Their apartment was a little small, a little dark, a little messy. It occupied part of the first floor of a brick rowhouse on the north side of South Philadelphia. Since her divorce, Cole and his mom had worked hard to make a cozy and loving home, a perfect nest for two.

They hadn't planned on all the visitors. Hadn't invited them. But still they came.

They came often and whenever they pleased. They never announced themselves, and they certainly weren't welcome. Only Cole could see them.

To their credit, they never bothered Lynn. They weren't interested in her, so she never even knew they were there.

They called, instead, on Cole.

But tonight, so far, they were silent.

CHAPTER 1

In Center City, Philadelphia, about one mile and a couple of tax brackets away from the Sears' neighborhood, Dr. Malcolm Crowe and his wife, Anna, lived in a townhouse with a wide, welcoming stoop. It was neither the smallest nor biggest house on the street, and it was known by the neighbors chiefly for the light that often burned all night in Malcolm's third-floor study.

In a city that crawled with psychotherapists, Dr. Crowe's name stood out. His success rate was legendary. His appointment book was full for months.

Lynn Sear had known about him for years.

So had nearly every other parent of a troubled child. Many called him in a panic, and most were politely referred to other therapists with less crowded schedules. But Lynn believed her son needed the best, and she'd been persistent. One month from now, Cole had an appointment to see Dr. Crowe, due to a last-minute cancellation. Dr. Crowe had already interviewed Lynn over the phone about her son. She knew she'd been lucky. Today Dr. Crowe had been honored in a public ceremony at city hall. With all the publicity, he would soon be unreachable.

That night, as Cole and Lynn slept, Anna Crowe descended into the basement and flicked on a light. It was a dank, dismal place, empty but for a well-stocked wine rack. She had always meant to do something about the space. It had potential.

Anna shivered. The room was awfully cold for an autumn night — a damp, wintry cold that sent a chill down her spine.

She glanced over the wine bottles. There. A Beaujolais Villages, good vintage, Malcolm's favorite.

As she raced back upstairs, she shut the door tight behind her.

Her husband was sprawled on the living room floor. He was thirty-eight years old but his smile had the confident glint of a man half his age, and his sturdy physique attested to regular weekend rowing on the Schuylkill River. The only signs of approaching mid-life were the lines on his face, lines that told of the sleepless nights he spent unraveling children's problems to which there were no simple answers.

Tonight Malcolm had vowed not to set foot in his study. Tonight he'd promised to celebrate.

Anna saw themselves as Inner and Outer people. As Malcolm was dedicated to the mind's deepest mysteries, Anna was dedicated to its artistic expression. Her antique gallery was small but it had a growing reputation. She'd saved some of her best work for their house, restoring every detail — the dark polish of the wainscoted wooden walls, the fiery facets of the crystal foyer chandelier, the delicate coziness of the Persian rugs. Malcolm refused to call it a restoration. He called it Annatomic Reconstruction.

Anna put the wine on the coffee table and slipped on a cardigan that had been hanging over a chair. She handed Malcolm a Liberty Rowing Club sweatshirt from the sofa. "It's getting cold," she said, curling up beside him as he dug the last piece of shrimp from a Chinese takeout container.

Both of them now faced Malcolm's latest award, an ivory vellum certificate framed in dark wood and propped on a chair opposite the coffee table.

"That's one fine frame," Malcolm said. "A fine frame it is. How much does a fine frame like that cost, you think?"

Anna loved when he was goofy like this. He hardly ever did it anymore. "I've never told you, but you sound a little like Dr. Seuss when you're happy."

"Anna, I'm serious," Malcolm said with a self-satisfied smile. "Serious I am, Anna."

Anna's trained eyes easily assessed the value and material of the frame. "Mahogany," she said decisively. "I'd say that cost at least a couple hundred. Maybe three."

"Three?" Malcolm's eyebrows shot up. "We should hock it — buy that CD rack for the bedroom."

A joke, as usual. That was just like Malcolm. Anything that pointed to his achievements became a joke. And he was charming enough to get away with it. What was the point? To keep himself humble? He was already humble. For all his hard work, for all his brilliant insights, for all the parents who cried their gratitude to him over the phone, for all the children whose drawings festooned the living room walls — for all of that, he should let himself reap a reward now and then.

Well, tonight he would. He deserved this award, and Anna was determined to let him know that. To let him *feel* it. "Do you know how important this is?" she asked. "This is big time. I am going to read this certificate for you."

"I sound like Dr. Seuss?" Malcolm leaned in to tickle her.

Anna deftly slid out of his reach. "'In recognition for his outstanding achievement in the field of psychology, his dedication to his work, and his continuing effort to improve the quality of life for countless children and their families, the city of Philadelphia proudly bestows upon its son, Dr. Malcolm Crowe' — that's you — 'the mayor's citation for professional excellence.' Wow . . . they called you their *son*."

Malcolm nodded. "We can keep it in the bathroom."

"This is an important night for us," Anna insisted. "Finally someone is recognizing the sacrifices you made — that you have put everything second, including me, for those families they're talking about."

Malcolm's hands drifted lightly, playfully, over her cheek. She hated reminding him about his "sacrifices." It was the only thing they ever fought about, really — the forgotten dinner dates, the chronic lateness, the last-minute cancellations. But it was the truth. They always told each other the truth. She knew what he was like before she'd married him. *For better or for worse,* they'd said. Overall, it had been worth it.

"They're also saying that my husband has a gift," Anna continued, taking his hand. "Not an ordinary gift that allows him to hit a ball over a fence, or a gift that lets him produce beautiful images on canvas. Your gift teaches children how to be strong in situations where most adults would piss on themselves. I believe what they wrote about you, Malcolm."

Her eyes were brimming with tears. Malcolm wrapped her in a soft embrace. "Thank you," he said.

"Sorry. There wasn't supposed to be any crying. This is a celebration."

Malcolm grinned. "I would like some red wine in a glass. I would not like it in a mug. I would not like it in a jug."

Anna broke out laughing.

He'd done it again.

She wanted to smack him.

She loved him.

They were giddy as they entered the bedroom. Giddy and playful. Anna danced, her light purple dress swinging as lazily as the room's indigo curtains in the autumn breeze.

For the millionth time Malcolm marveled that she had ever agreed to marry him. In the soft bedroom light, she was exquisite. She was always exquisite. Her skin had the translucence of pearl, her hair a liquid-brown richness that framed her face in the shape of a heart. She was teasing him with her eyes — eyes that could be both playful and fierce, intelligent and patient, open and direct yet full of silent, unanswerable mysteries. In their years of marriage Anna had never looked at him the same way twice. She kept things exciting.

Tonight she was in a good mood. But she was cold, too, and the wind was brisk, so Malcolm turned to shut the window.

He stopped when he saw the shattered glass.

The window lay in jagged shards on the

floor, trailing into the room along the carpet. Nearby the bedroom lamp had been knocked over and broken. Instantly, their playful word was *shattered*—just like the window. An icy cold chill ran through their veins. They knew.

Anna stopped dancing. "He's still in the house," she whispered.

From behind them, a shadow slid across the floor. Anna screamed.

Malcolm spun around. The bathroom light was on.

Carefully he moved closer. A black shirt lay on the porcelain tiles. Black pants. Unfamiliar clothes.

Talk to him, Malcolm said to himself. *Be calm. Show no fear. Don't threaten.*

Before Malcolm reached the bathroom, a man stepped into the light. The intruder.

He was a young man of nineteen or twenty, wearing nothing but a pair of white briefs. His body was emaciated and covered with angry scars, his lower lip split by a recent wound. His brown hair, dirty and matted down, had a streak of white at the left temple. Like a meek, guilty child, he stopped stiffly in front of the sink, with bowed head and clasped hands.

Show no fear.

"Anna, don't move," Malcolm said. "Don't say a word." Evenly, calmly, he addressed the young man. "This is Forty-seven Locust Street. You have broken a window and entered a private residence. Do you understand what I'm saying?"

The man looked up. His eyes were glazed and jumpy, in a haggard face twisted with rage.

The voice, however, was what scared Malcolm most. It was the choked, pleading voice of utter despair, a cry supported by words. "You don't know so many things."

I know this voice. I know this desperation. How many times have I seen it?

"There are no needles or prescription drugs of any kind in this house —"

The man turned his crazed, imploring eyes on Anna. "Do you know why you're scared when you're alone?" His face suddenly crumpled, his lips quivering. "I do . . ."

"What do you want?" Anna blurted out.

"What *he* promised!" the man shot back, pointing at Malcolm.

"My God," Anna gasped.

Malcolm looked closely at the man's face. Something was familiar. "Do I know you?"

"I was ten when you worked with me," the

man said with bitterness. "Downtown clinic? Single parent family? I had a possible mood disorder. I had no friends. You said I was socially isolated. I was afraid. You called it acute anxiety disorder. *You were wrong!*"

Malcolm stepped back. The profile — he knew the profile. He thought back — when? About a decade ago, perhaps . . . *There were so many faces, so many stones . . .*

"I'm nineteen," the stranger went on. "I have drugs in my system twenty-four hours a day. I still have no friends. I still have no peace. I'm still afraid." He paused, choking back a sob. "I'm still afraid."

"Please give me a second to think." Malcolm's fingers shook as he touched his chin. *Ten years old. Nine years ago. Those eyes . . .* "Ben Friedkin?"

"Some people called me Freak."

"Ronald? Ronald Sumner?"

"I *am* a Freak."

Freak. That name. There was a boy back then. A sweet, troubled, difficult case. *The boy who always wore a scarf, even in summer . . .* "Vincent — Vincent Gray?"

Surprise shot across the man's eyes.

Malcolm exhaled with relief. "I do remember

you, Vincent," he said gently. "You were a good kid. Very smart . . . quiet . . . compassionate. Unusually compassionate."

"You forgot *cursed*!" Tears streamed down Vincent's face. *"You failed me!"*

Calm him down. Talk to him.

"Vincent, I'm sorry I didn't help you. I can try to help you now."

Vincent turned abruptly. His right hand reached into the sink, and he pulled out a gun.

Malcolm recoiled. Vincent aimed.

The shot shattered the peace of the autumn night. Malcolm fell back onto the bed, clutching his stomach. Anna shrieked in horror.

As she kneeled over her husband, Vincent pointed the gun to his own head and pulled the trigger.

CHAPTER 2

It seemed as if no time had passed at all. But it was a year later, and the trees were brilliant with the changing season.

Malcolm seldom thought about that awful day anymore, about the sound of the gunshot and the way it had changed everything. But he was still a psychologist — despite the horror and bloodshed, he could not stop feeling responsible for Vincent Gray. For all Malcolm's success, he had failed the boy.

Now fate, it seemed, had given him an opportunity to try again.

As he sat on a bench across from a line of brick rowhouses, he reviewed the problems of an intriguing case. It was one of the many he had never been able to follow up on. He vaguely remembered talking to Mrs. Sear. She had been especially eager for her son to see Malcolm as soon as possible.

He could see why.

Malcolm ran his finger down the notes he'd taken of their phone conversation over a year ago. He'd circled all the relevant phrases: *Acute anxiety . . . socially isolated . . . possible mood disorder . . . parental status — divorced . . . communication difficulty between mother–child dyad.*

The symptoms were the same, word for word, as Vincent's.

He was nervous about this. He could feel Anna's anger and frustration, the tension that had always existed between them. She thought she was second in Malcolm's mind; she'd told him so.

It wasn't true, of course. But he had a job, he was passionate about it, and he'd been away from it for a long time. In the end, she had always understood that part of him. He hoped she still did.

A life might depend on this case. Perhaps this time, he would do some good. Perhaps he could head off a tragedy before it happened. He didn't know exactly how — but then again, you never went into a patient relationship with answers. First you listened.

As the rowhouse door slowly creaked open, Malcolm looked up.

The boy appeared, peering cautiously into the street. He was small for eight, his hands barely reaching the knob. His glasses certainly didn't help; they were at least three sizes too large.

Malcolm stuffed his notes in his briefcase, then stood up to cross the street's center median.

But the boy was gone, racing down the brick sidewalk as fast as his little legs could carry him. Had he seen Malcolm?

Malcolm gave chase. The boy turned right at the corner. He dodged into a parking lot at the end of the block.

The lot led through the block to the next street, where a large brick church stood. Cole was yanking at the handles, throwing his entire body into opening the solid oak door. He seemed frantic, scared.

Resistance. Not uncommon in a child this age.

Malcolm took a deep breath and followed.

Inside, the church was nearly empty, save for one worshipper in the back and a row of toy soldiers lining the top of a pew in the middle.

Malcolm quietly sat in the pew behind the soldiers. A tiny hand reached up and placed a knight beside a king.

"Deprofundi . . . clamad . . . Domine . . ." Cole was muttering something barely intelligible. Latin, it sounded like.

Don't scare him. Just make conversation.

"You know something about churches?" Malcolm said. "In olden times, in Europe, people used to hide in churches to claim sanctuary."

Cole peered over the pew. His face was small, a bit pinched, his chin tapering to a point. His hair needed a trim, and it looked as though he'd gotten white paint on the back of his head.

But Malcolm was transfixed by the boy's extraordinary eyes. They assessed him through lensless glasses, brown and soulful, with the sad gravity of someone ten times his age.

Malcolm was fairly certain Cole would bolt. Instead the boy spoke up in a small voice: "What were they hiding from?"

"Oh, lots of things, I suppose," Malcolm answered. "Bad people, for one. People who wanted to imprison them, hurt them."

"Nothing bad can happen in a church, right?"

Malcolm couldn't answer that honestly. He didn't want to put a chink in the boy's faith. As long as Cole was capable of faith and hope, he could be helped. "Your eyeglass frames," Malcolm said. "They don't seem to have any lenses in them."

"They're my dad's. The lenses hurt my eyes."

"I knew there was a sound explanation," Malcolm said with a warm smile. *Definite father issues*. "What was that you were saying before with your soldiers? Day . . . pro . . . fun —"

"*De profundis clamo ad te Domine*," Cole said. "It's called Latin. It's a language."

Malcolm was impressed. The kid was intelligent. "All your soldiers speak Latin?"

"No, just one." Cole eyed Malcolm intently. "Are you a good doctor?" he finally asked.

The kid's perceptive, too. "I got an award once. From the mayor. It had an expensive frame."

Cole nodded. "That's pretty good."

"Thank you. It was a long time ago. I've been kind of retired for awhile. You're my first client back."

As the boy began to pocket his action figures, Malcolm caught a glimpse of his arms. They were covered with a dense crosshatch of cuts and bruises, some clearly recent and still angry.

Malcolm had to catch his breath. This was like Vincent, too.

Cole stood up. "I'm going to see you again, right?"

"If it's okay with you," Malcolm replied.

Without answering, Cole stepped into the aisle and walked toward the altar, heading toward an exit on the left.

Malcolm watched him go, focusing on the patch of white paint at the tip of his hair.

It wasn't paint. It was a streak of white hair.

Cole picked up his pace. Just before he veered to the exit, he swiped a small religious figurine from the altar.

Malcolm turned up Locust Street, pensive and distracted. Cole seemed intelligent, quiet, sensitive. The boy's fantasies were richly active but seemed to be age-appropriate.

But children like Cole were full of surprises, Malcolm knew. The kleptomania was troubling.

And, of course, the scars. They could be marks from rough playground antics, who knew? He didn't seem to be an athletic type, though.

This boy headed to a church when he was afraid. He craved sanctuary. Protection. From what? Was his mother attacking him? Not likely — why would she have set up the appointment? The kids at school, perhaps. Surely a boy his size and temperament would be picked on.

But bullies generally began inflicting serious physical injury at a later age — fifth or sixth grade, not third.

Perhaps Cole was injuring himself.

Malcolm would have to visit the school. Observe the mother in the home. Things he may not have done sufficiently ten years ago.

The parallels were uncanny — right down to the patch of white hair. There had to be an explanation, some connection Malcolm was missing.

This case was going to need a long time and a lot of energy.

At number 47 he bounded up the stoop and unlocked the front door. The entrance hall was dimly lit, and a mountain of mail stood precariously on a table. At the top of the stairway, a soft light shone from the bedroom. Anna was home.

"It's me!" he called out.

No answer.

He took off his jacket and tie, tossing them on the sofa. The dining room table had been set for one. A meal sat half finished on the plate.

She wasn't waiting for him for dinner anymore. They always used to eat together.

Anna, he knew, was afraid. She didn't want to go through such a trauma again. Malcolm-back-to-work meant Malcolm-leaving-himself-open-to-homicidal-maniacs. She was depressed, too, that life would be going back to the way it was: Anna returning from the antique shop at precisely the same time each night to an empty house. Or worse, Anna finding the man of her dreams absorbed in the study of the minds of children who grow up and sometimes return for vengeance.

Anna's patience was crumbling.

Vincent Gray had changed everything.

Malcolm ascended the stairs and walked quietly into the bedroom. His wife was asleep, curled up on her side. Her reading lamp was still aglow.

In her right hand she clutched a wad of tissues, still wet with tears. She looked like a mournful angel. He didn't have the heart to wake her. She was so peaceful now. She didn't deserve to be angry.

Malcolm backed out of the bedroom. He had the urge to retire to his study, which was now in the basement.

He slipped downstairs and tried the basement door. It was locked.

She was angry, too.

Working in the basement was not a pleasant experience. Malcolm had no shelves, his desk was crammed against the wine rack, and his stuff had been scattered helter skelter over everything.

From a pile of old books, he pulled out his Latin dictionary. He hadn't used it since college, and a layer of dust fell away as he opened it.

He placed his notebook beside it on the desk and read what he'd transcribed in church — Cole's phrase: *De profundis clamo ad te Domine.*

Flipping through the dictionary, he translated each word.

Out of the depths, I cry to you, Lord.

Malcolm recognized this.

It was from the mass for the dead.

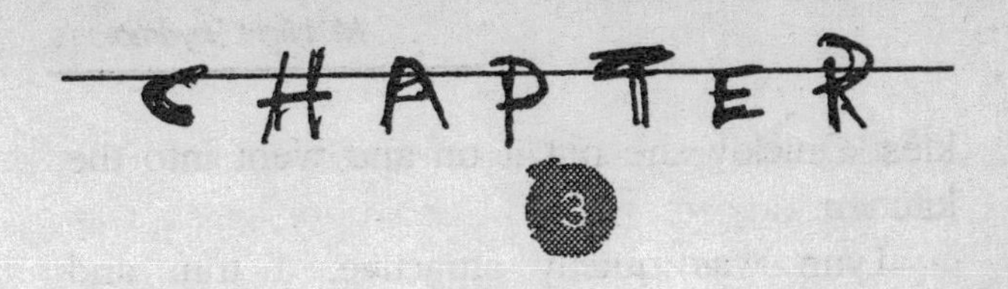

". . . and it's fifty-four degrees in South Philly on this cloudy Monday morning, with a chance of rain later today. In this morning's head-lines —"

Lynn Sear switched off the radio on top of the clothes dryer. It was too late to be distracted by the news. She was running behind schedule as always, and her only clean tops were in the laundry basket.

Unfortunately so was Sebastian, Cole's puppy. Fast asleep.

She pulled out a black blouse, temporarily waking the lazy beast, and shook out the wrinkles. Quickly she put it on and went into the kitchen.

Lynn was quietly attractive, a trim and young-looking woman with wavy brown hair that her friends claimed to admire, although she described it as mousy. Her motions were efficient and quick, but her eyes had the calmness of a woman who knew her place in the world and made the most of it.

Although she'd left the kitchen spotless the night before, it was already a mess. Cole's cereal, puffed and bloated with milk, sat in a bowl on the small table. The utensil drawer and two cupboard doors were open. Cole was in his room, getting dressed.

Lynn shook her head. One of these days he'd learn to do these things in the right order.

"Cole?" she called out.

She adored her son. Everything she did, every thought in her long day revolved around the question, *What's best for Cole?* Theirs was a single-parent home, but the love they shared more than made up for her husband's departure. But Cole missed his father deeply, and that broke Lynn's heart — because frankly, Ken Sear was a major-league creep. Right now, as she scrambled to make ends meet, he was probably snug in his little Pittsburgh apartment, being served bacon and eggs by Trudy the Toll Collector, the woman he'd run off with.

No matter. Life was too short for bitterness. They made a good family, Cole and she. Lynn would give him all the attention he craved and every opportunity he needed. Affording the tuition to St. Anthony's Academy was a constant struggle, but worth every penny. He would grow up among good, thoughtful, educated people. He would even show them a thing or two. He was that kind of kid.

If only it were that easy.

She had long ago given up trying to predict Cole's behavior. One minute he was focused and happy, the next moment shaking like a reed in the wind. The screaming at night, the clammy hands — that was all supposed to have gone away after the divorce. That was what the priests and psychologists had said. But they'd been wrong.

The cuts and bruises were the worst. Some of them he must have given himself. He'd wake up with them in the morning, and she knew they hadn't been there the previous day. The shrinks and priests had an answer for that, too. Plenty of kids scratch themselves in their sleep, they said.

But so savagely? she would ask. Cole wasn't capable of such ferocity.

"He'll grow out of it" was about the best they could do. Big help.

Something was wrong. Terribly wrong.

Whatever it was, she was determined to hold up her end. She needed to bolster his self-esteem. To listen and love. To get him the best help and stick with him until he was better.

It was the only way she knew how.

She knew she had to be strong and alert. Right at this moment, that meant a good strong cup of coffee.

She quickly closed the drawer and cabinets and pulled out the coffeemaker. Her hands were shaking as she poured the water. Suddenly it felt freezing in here.

Turning around, she jacked up the thermostat.

Cole was standing in the kitchen doorway, dressed in his St. Anthony's uniform — blazer, khaki pants, clip-on tie. He looked almost neat.

As he sat at the table, Lynn said to him,

"Your Cocoa Puffs are getting soggy." Her sharp mother's-eyes zeroed right in on a grease stain on his tie. "You got a spot."

In a quick, practiced series of motions, she unclipped his tie, stepped into the laundry room, threw the tie in the washing machine, and pulled a clean tie out of the dryer.

When she moved back into the kitchen, she nearly fainted.

The cupboards and drawers — *every one of them from top to bottom* — had been flung open.

Cole was sitting stiffly, exactly where he'd been a moment ago. His face was pale, his little hands pressed palm-down on the Formica table.

Lynn swallowed. How did he do that? She hadn't been out of the kitchen more than a few seconds. She squashed her rising panic.

"Something you were looking for, baby?" she asked gently.

"Pop-Tarts," Cole said, his eyes averted.

Lynn looked into an open food cabinet. The box of Pop-Tarts stood face-out on the second shelf. "They're right here."

"Oh."

She took the box and held it out to him.

Cole still wouldn't meet her glance. "What

are you thinking, Mama?" he asked. He couldn't mask the fear in his voice.

"Lots of things," Lynn replied, as nonchalantly as she could.

"Anything bad about me?"

Lynn leaned close, her elbows on the table, so that she was eye to eye with him. "Look at my face."

Cole turned warily toward her.

"I wasn't thinking anything bad about you," she said with soft conviction. "Got it?"

It was the simple truth. Life was too full of people who were willing to bring you down. But not in this house.

Not ever.

"Got it," Cole said, a little more confidence settling his voice.

The doorbell interrupted their conversation.

"That's Tommy, Mama." Cole stood up, kissed his mother on the cheek, and raced to the front door.

"Don't you want this?" Lynn held out a Pop-Tart.

Cole stopped in his tracks. He turned back, tentatively took the Pop-Tart, and left.

Lynn glanced at the kitchen table.

The sweaty remains of two small palm prints slowly began to evaporate.

Cole bounded down the stairs to the brick sidewalk, where Tommy Tammisimo stood waiting. Tommy was also eight but looked at least a year older. He was tall and solidly built, with neatly cut dark brown hair. He always seemed to be wearing brand-new clothes, and when he smiled he had two holes in his face which the grownups called dimples.

Tommy had been in a dumb TV commercial. Tommy thought he was hot stuff.

With a big, too-friendly smile, he took Cole's book bag and slung it over his shoulder. Flinging an arm around Cole, he turned back to the house and waved cheerily to Lynn, who was watching from the living room window.

At the end of the block, safely out of Lynn's sight, Tommy let go of Cole's shoulder and dumped the book bag back in his arms. "Hey, Freak, how'd you like the arm-around-your-shoulder bit?" he said with a cocky grin. "I just made it up. That's what great actors do. It's called improv."

Tommy began sprinting ahead toward school.

Looking back, he called out, "Be careful! I hope no one jumps out and gets you!"

Very funny.

Cole looked to his right, at the street's bushy center median, then to his left, at the evergreen near the corner. Cautiously he resumed his walk to school.

He was the last to arrive. As the other kids scampered in to beat the morning bell, Cole stood alone in the empty, leaf-strewn street.

St. Anthony's was a broad, sturdy building with stout columns flanking the front doors and fancy inscriptions that spoke of justice and democracy. It was one of the oldest structures in South Philly, built originally as a courthouse.

Cole knew a lot about its history. Perhaps a little too much. The place scared him. The kids scared him.

Shoving his hands in his pockets, he fingered his toy soldiers. Then he said a quick prayer and walked inside.

CHAPTER 4

When Cole arrived home from school that afternoon, Malcolm was waiting. He sat on a worn but comfortable brown-fabric chair with a small protective plastic mat to lean his head on. Lynn sat opposite him in an almost-matching chair, and a modest coffee table stood between them. Cole's toys had been lined up against the baseboards and on the windowsills. They spilled out of old boxes and hung off shelves. It was a friendly place, Malcolm thought, a bit cramped but tidy and clean. Clearly Cole had the run of the house, a healthy thing for an eight-year-old.

Cole walked inside, his body drooping and

face slightly downcast, the way he had walked out of the church.

When he saw Malcolm, he froze up and looked away.

Lynn stood from her chair and walked toward her son. "How was school, baby?"

Cole shrugged.

"You know," Lynn continued, kneeling to his level, "you can tell me things if you need to."

Malcolm noticed that Cole was refusing to look at him. The boy was staring at his mother with an awkward intensity.

"Well," Lynn said with a sudden, impish grin, "you know what *I* did today?"

Cole shook his head no.

She thought for a moment. "I . . . won the Pennsylvania lottery in the morning. I quit my jobs. I ate a big picnic in the park with lots of chocolate mousse pie, and then swam in the fountain all afternoon. What did *you* do?"

A smile started to creep across Cole's face. He and his mom had been doing this for as long as he'd been going to school. It never failed to cheer him up. "I was picked first for kickball teams at recess," he began. "I hit a grand slam to win the game, and everyone lifted me up on their shoulders and carried me around, cheering."

Lynn's expression was warm and cheerful, but Malcolm could detect the weight of a mother's pain — the knowledge that her son's deepest fantasy was about *acceptance.* And that he saw it as an unattainable dream.

"I'll make triangle pancakes," she said, taking his book bag and coat and heading toward the kitchen. "You got an hour."

Cole looked frail and sickly as he stood in the archway that separated the living room from the front foyer. Malcolm gestured to the chair Lynn had vacated. "You want to sit?"

The boy shook his head.

Malcolm had expected this. Cole saw this visit as a violation of his space. That was normal. Malcolm would have to make him feel at ease. Just go with him. Keep it light. No demands. "Don't feel like talking right now?" he asked jovially.

Again Cole shook his head.

"How about we play a game first?"

Cole's head remained still. This was progress.

"It's a mind-reading game," Malcolm went on. "Did I mention I could read minds? Here's the game. I'll read your mind. If what I say is right, you take a step toward the chair. If I'm wrong, you take a step back toward the doorway. If you reach the chair, you sit. If you reach the door, you can go. Deal?"

Cole looked puzzled but intrigued. He nodded yes.

Bingo.

This was one of Malcolm's best tactics. Kids enjoyed it. He almost always won, too, because every child unwittingly gave clues. Cole's wariness, Malcolm decided, hinted at a bad experience with psychotherapists.

He sat back and closed his eyes. Pressing his fingers to his forehead, he let out a soft, high-pitched drone and then said, "Just after your mom and dad were divorced, your mom went to a doctor like me and it didn't help her. And so . . . you think I'm not going to help you."

Malcolm opened his eyes. Cole stood still for a second, his brow scrunched up. Then he took a step forward, his feet soundless on the speckled acrylic throw rug.

Repeating the mystical routine, Malcolm proclaimed, "You're worried because she said she told him things — things she couldn't tell anybody else. Secrets."

Cole took another step forward, off the rug and onto the wood floor.

This time Malcolm looked at him levelly. "You have a secret. But you don't want to tell me."

Another step. If he took one more, he would be at the chair.

Cole looked scared and shaky, so Malcolm tried to put him at ease. "You don't have to tell me your secret if you don't want to."

As he lifted his fingers to his forehead again, he noticed an adult-sized watch hanging loosely on Cole's wrist. "Your father gave you that watch as a present before he left."

Thump. Cole took a step back. "He forgot it in a drawer," the boy explained. "It doesn't work."

Okay. Time to focus on the boy's overt personality traits. His shyness. His articulate speech and knowledge of Latin. "You don't like to say much at school," Malcolm tried. "You're an excellent student, however. You've never been in any kind of serious trouble."

One more step back, onto the rug. "We were supposed to draw a picture — anything we wanted," Cole explained, quietly — almost desperately. "I drew a man. He got hurt in the neck by another man with a screwdriver."

Violent fantasies. That hadn't been part of the profile.

But it made sense.

Malcolm reminded himself it was too early to jump to conclusions. Often, in sensitive children, dark visions were brought on by disturbing media images.

"You saw that on TV, Cole?" Malcolm asked.

Cole stepped back again. He had taken back all his ground. He was one step from the door.

"Everyone got upset. They had a meeting. Mama started crying." Cole's voice was unusual. It was flat, matter-of-fact, tinged with sadness, with none of the lilting timbre and diffuse mumbling typical of most children his age. "I don't draw like that anymore."

"How do you draw now?" Malcolm asked.

"I draw people smiling, dogs running, and rainbows." Cole paused. They don't have meetings about rainbows."

Malcolm nodded. "I guess they don't."

Cole stood rock-still, staring curiously at Malcolm. "What am I thinking now?" the boy challenged him.

"You're thinking . . ." Malcolm was at a loss. This wasn't the right game for a boy with Cole's mind. He didn't follow the patterns. He projected fragility and helplessness, the beaten-down quality of someone who has discovered life's cruel limits. He knew how to manipulate adults and had learned not to expect their help. Yet help was what he needed, big time. Help and truth. "I don't know what you're thinking, Cole."

Cole stepped back, into the front vestibule. "I was thinking, you're nice," he said softly. "But you can't help me."

With that, he was gone. Cole's words, barely above a whisper, hung in the air. Thin and reedy, and steeped in confusion and fear.

The game was over.

The work had just begun. Malcolm had come so close . . . he wanted to help so badly. The boy had slipped away . . . but Malcolm would not let him go.

Malcolm looked at his watch as he barged into La Bella Luna Restaurant.

Eight-thirty.

He wanted to kick himself. The Sear case had consumed his entire evening — the meeting with Cole, then four solid hours in his study.

And for what? He was more confused than ever. Plus he was an hour late for his wedding anniversary dinner. Of all days.

Anna was going to kill him. This was exactly

the kind of thing she hated most. It made all her worst accusations true.

Malcolm wouldn't blame her. She'd always told him he couldn't manage time well, and she was right. Cute youthful habits did not wear well into middle age. They turned into thoughtlessness and passive-aggressive behavior. But Anna was human. And neither of them was getting any younger. Too little time together was too little time together.

He spotted Anna exactly where he expected her to be. She was sitting at the same table where they'd sat when he'd proposed to her. That night he had made sure to bribe the maître d' in advance to reserve it. It was in the quietest, most romantic spot of the restaurant, near a leafy potted plant, with a view of the magnificent wrought-iron entrance. Tonight she was alone. Malcolm's place setting had been removed. A plate of chocolate cake sat untouched in front of her, lit by the small table lamp.

She adored chocolate cake. She adored all food. She only stopped eating when she was upset.

Malcolm doubted she'd even touched her salad tonight.

He walked to the table and took a deep

breath. When all was lost, he figured, use humor. "I thought you meant the *other* Italian restaurant I asked you to marry me in," he said.

Anna ignored the joke.

"I'm so sorry," Malcolm said, dropping the façade. "I can't seem to keep track of time. It didn't go well today. I spent some time after trying to get my head together."

Anna brusquely signaled the waiter.

Malcolm sat opposite her. "They're so *similar,* Anna. They have the same mannerisms, the same expressions — the same *thing* hanging over them. It might be some kind of abuse."

Anna flashed him a quick glance, but he felt as if she were looking right through him.

"There are cuts on Cole's arms," Malcolm continued. "Fingernail marks, I think. They look like defensive cuts — possibly a teacher, a neighbor. I don't think it's the mother. That's just a gut thing — the way she deals with him, it doesn't fit." He shrugged. "It's hard to say this early. Could just be a kid climbing a lot of trees."

The waiter breezed by, placing a check on the table. Malcolm reached for it, but Anna snatched it away before he could touch it. She signed it right away and pushed back her chair.

"I know I've been kind of distracted, and I

know it makes you mad," Malcolm said, "but I'm getting a second chance. I can't let it slip away."

Anna waited until he was finished before standing up. "Happy anniversary," she said bitterly, walking away.

Malcolm remained at the table, his head in his hands, as her footsteps receded into the distance.

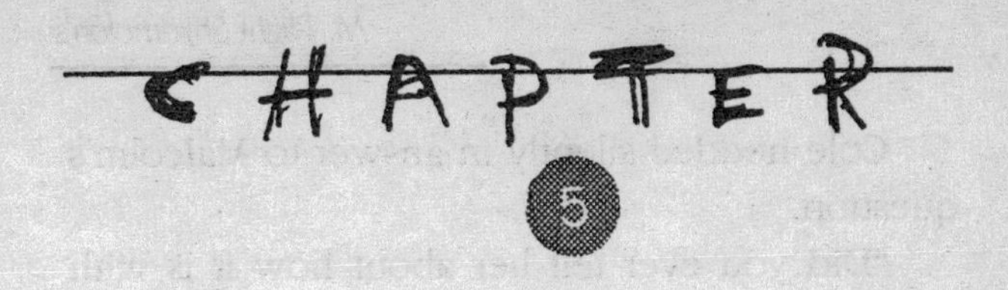

CHAPTER 5

"I walk this way to school with Tommy Tammisimo," Cole explained the next day, heading left out of his house.

Malcolm nodded, falling in stride with him on the brick sidewalk. "Is he your best friend?"

"He hates me."

"Do you hate him?"

Cole shook his head.

"Your mom set that up?"

A soccer team passed in front of them, boys not much older than Cole, boisterous and carefree and happy. The way Cole ought to be.

No one said hi.

Cole nodded silently in answer to Malcolm's question.

"Did you ever tell her about how it is with Tommy?" Malcolm asked.

"I don't tell her things," Cole replied.

"Why?"

"Because she doesn't look at me the way everybody else does, and I don't want her to. I don't want her to know."

"Know what?"

"That I'm a freak."

That name. That awful, demeaning name.

"Listen to me," Malcolm said firmly. "You are not a freak. Don't believe anybody that tells you that." Malcolm used a curse, telling Cole he didn't have to grow up believing he was a freak. Cole was surprised and impressed — not by the advice, but by the curse.

At the four-way stop sign, they turned right.

Cole showed Malcolm the school and the playground. Afterward they walked around the neighborhood and Cole pointed out highlights. Then they swung by the "nice" neighborhood, where the houses were bigger and fancier. Cole pointed out Tommy's home.

They didn't accomplish much that afternoon, but Malcolm hadn't expected to. After the stiff formality of the first meeting, he needed to gain the boy's trust, to put him at ease. When Cole relaxed a bit, he was kind and well-mannered, observant and thoughtful. And, clearly gifted. He had a bright future in store — if he could make it through the present.

That night Malcolm fell asleep in his office, his head buried in a book called *The Tormented Child*.

The next day, Lynn Sear had the morning shift off. This meant she could see Cole off to school, clean the house, and do the laundry before she had to leave. She slipped on the earphones of her Walkman, turned up the volume, and went about her chores.

The house was cold again. Unusually cold. She turned up the thermostat as she swept through the rooms, collecting dirty clothes in her laundry basket. A pair of socks and a T-shirt lay on the floor beneath the "Hall of Fame," Cole's nickname for the wall that was decorated floor to ceiling with family photos. She stooped to pick up the clothes, lingering for a moment to recapture the fading memories that beamed out from the wall. Just about every picture had Cole at the center, as it should. She especially loved an image of Cole as a three-year-old, smiling almost defiantly, as if nothing could ever make him sad. He left his clothes around the house back then, too.

Her eye focused on a slight flare to the left of Cole's face, a semicircle of light against a vertical tangent. It seemed to be moving, as if the camera had caught a tiny floating Tinkerbell off guard.

A reflection of the sun against the lens, she guessed.

But as she looked from photo to photo — Cole at his two-year birthday party, Cole under the Christmas tree at age five, Cole and Lynn at Hersheypark, at the neighborhood barbecue, in the swimming pool — she saw the glare in each one. Both indoor and outdoor shots. And it was always in the same place, just beside Cole's face.

Odd. She'd have to get the camera checked.

Lynn tore herself away and bustled into Cole's room. It was, as always, a wreck. A shame, because although it was small, it really was the nicest room in the house. The walls were paneled with the original dark-stained wood, solid and masculine. Over the years Lynn had collected lovely antique furniture and lighting. She'd hung up all of Cole's beautiful paintings of happy families and pretty houses and arching rainbows. He loved to draw rainbows.

She had to step around Cole's makeshift tent just inside the door, a rickety thing made of old red bedsheets, propped up with bamboo sticks and held together with clothespins. A handwritten sign, DO NOT ENTER, hung crookedly over the entrance flap.

She'd just as soon get rid of it, but she didn't dare. Cole cherished the space inside. It was his special private place to be by himself, where no one could bother him—and if it made him happy, so be it.

Cole's desk, however, was a public disaster, with papers strewn all over. She began tidying up with her free hand, when she noticed a page covered with dark, jagged writing.

She leaned closer to look.

The words covered the entire page. They were in Cole's handwriting, but as if he'd written with pen in fist, up and down and sideways, scribbling against time, never taking his hand from the page—angry words, foul words. . . .

. . . Christ, break the freaking glass oh no God what the hell is going on QUIET THE DAMN BABY I'LL CUT YOU I SWEAR IT someone stop the

burning I'LL KILL YOU I'LL KILL ALL YOU BASTARDS. . . .

Lynn dropped the laundry basket.

Malcolm visited the house after school that afternoon. Cole avoided him, playing with his action figures behind the sofa. Malcolm asked a few leading questions, about Cole's life, his dad, the divorce, and the move to this apartment. The boy answered politely but briefly.

The violent writings would have to be eased into the conversation.

Rain pelted the living room windows, and the room felt stuffy. Malcolm struggled to be comfortable as he listened, periodically seeing the top of a blue winter hat and a little hand reaching up to commandeer a knight into battle.

"So your dad lives in Pittsburgh," Malcolm said, "with a lady who works in a toll booth."

"What if she has to pee when she's working?" Cole piped up from behind the sofa. "You think she just holds it?"

"I don't know. I was just thinking the same thing."

Cole dive-bombed some kind of action figure into something on the floor and made various exploding noises. Malcolm looked at his watch. "You're asking a lot of questions about Dad today," Cole finally remarked. "How come?"

"Sometimes, even though we don't know it, we do things to draw attention — do things so we can express how we feel about issues, divorce or whatever."

"Nyyyyeaoo . . . psssssh . . . aggghhh!"

Cole's voice was soft, muffled. Malcolm had no idea if he was listening. He continued, measuring his words carefully: "One might, as an example, leave something on a desk for someone to find."

The boy's head stopped moving. He fell silent.

"Cole," Malcolm said, "have you ever heard of something called free writing — or free-association writing?"

Cole's hat shook slowly from side to side.

"It's when you put a pencil in your hand and put the pencil to a paper, and you just start writing," Malcolm explained. "You don't think about what you're writing, you don't read what you're writing — you just keep your hand moving. After awhile, if you keep your hand moving long enough, words and thoughts start coming out that you didn't even know you had in you. Sometimes they're things you heard from somewhere. Sometimes they're feelings deep inside."

Malcolm paused to let the words sink in. He kept a close eye on Cole's hat, protruding over the top of the sofa. It was rock-still.

"Have you ever done any free-association writing, Cole?" Malcolm asked.

Cole's hat bobbed up and down. A yes.

"What did you write?"

"Words."

"What kind of words?"

"Upset words."

"Did you ever write any upset words before your father left?"

"I don't remember."

Enough. Malcolm knew he couldn't press too hard, couldn't make himself the enemy. He would have to plant seeds, draw Cole out gradually. The most important thing you learned as a child psychologist was when to stop.

"Can you do something for me?" Malcolm asked, standing to grab his coat. "Think about what you want from our time together — what our goal should be."

He could see Cole now, crouched on the floor. The hat surrounded the boy's face, with two Velcro flaps attached under his chin. "Something *I* want?" he asked.

Malcolm smiled. It was such a strange concept to some kids, that a therapeutic relationship should help *them*. "If we could change something in your life, anything at all, what would it be?"

Cole frowned, searching his mind for an answer as if this were a math test.

"You don't have to answer now," Malcolm said, turning for the door.

"Instead of something I want, can I have something I don't want?"

Malcolm turned back. Cole was standing beside the sofa now. He was dressed in his dad's jacket, which draped to the floor.

Giving the boy a nod, Malcolm waited for the answer. Cole's eyes were sunken and sad as he screwed up the courage to speak.

"I don't want to be scared anymore."

CHAPTER 6

The textbook print swam before Malcolm's eyes. It was late morning — exactly *how* late, he was afraid to check. He'd been down in the basement for a long while now. It seemed he lived down here these days.

He rubbed his eyes and scanned the page — a diagnosis of a personality profile similar in many ways to Vincent's and Cole's.

A phrase at the bottom of the page jumped out at him. He took his pen and circled it:

. . . with the presenting symptoms in children of this type, the resulting bruises and abrasions on arms and legs may, in fact, be self-inflicted.

It made sense. Sort of. He'd thought about it many times. But somehow he couldn't believe it.

Maybe Vincent developed a self-destructive streak as he grew into adolescence. But as a child? He was like Cole, meek and small and cerebral. The writings were one thing — a healthy outlet, perhaps, for the violent thoughts. But it was a long leap from thought to action. And Malcolm just didn't buy that it had happened.

The doorbell sounded from upstairs.

Malcolm looked upward. "Are you going to get that?" he called out.

Anna's footsteps clattered across the hallway floor, just above him. Malcolm stood, stretching his legs, shaking out the mental cobwebs.

"What, you don't see enough of me at the store?" his wife's voice filtered down through the floor.

"I'm on my way out to the flea market in Amish country," a male voice answered.

Malcolm didn't recognize the voice, but he knew the type, just from the sound of it. Some brainy just-out-of-college art major willing to work at minimum wage to show off his knowledge of Louis XIV love seats to Mainline Philly bluebloods. "Thought you might want to come," the guy continued. "You could show me how to buy at these things."

"I trust you," Anna replied. "Besides, I don't know if I'm up for the Amish today. You can't curse or spit or anything around them."

Malcolm smiled. She may have been furious at him, but she hadn't lost her light touch.

"I thought you might want to get out," the man continued. "You've been kind of down."

Malcolm's smile vanished.

"That's very sweet," Anna said. "I'm okay."

"Do you think I should stop by on my way back, show you what I got? It's not a problem."

Not a problem? The woman is married, you pinhead! Malcolm wanted to shout. The nerve of this guy.

"You know, that's probably not the best idea, Sean," Anna said gently. "I'll just wait to see them in the store."

"Okay," Sean replied nervously. "Fine. Understood. . . . I'm off, then."

"Don't step in the horse manure."

"Thanks!"

The front door thumped shut. Malcolm moved across the basement to look out the street-side window. A young, dark-haired man jogged from the house to an SUV parked at the curb. He couldn't be more than twenty-five, thin and skittish-looking, an artsy self-conscious type.

Sean turned suddenly from the car and lurched a step back toward the house, his face pained, as if he'd just blown an important meeting. Then, stopping himself, he spun back around, pounded the hood in frustration, and jumped in.

Malcolm shook his head. "Give it up, kid," he murmured.

CHAPTER 7

Cole was bored. Mr. Cunningham had a way of doing that to a class.

On the side blackboard, Bobby O'Donnell scribbled *I will not hit or kick anyone* over and over. Bobby was bored, too. He was a pretty good kid, not as mean as the others — but when he was teased, he fought back, and Mr. Cunningham did not like any disruptions in class.

Mr. Cunningham wasn't an awful teacher, not old and tired and ugly like Mrs. Hoogstratten in math class. Just boring. He looked exactly the same every day — perfect and neat, kind of like a window mannequin. He was thin and he spoke slowly and carefully. That made sense, because when he was a kid, he had a speech problem. One of the old teachers, Mrs. Deems, had confided that to Cole. She wasn't around anymore, but she'd taught Mr. Cunningham when *he* was a third-grader at St. Anthony's. Anyway, aside from teaching social studies, Mr. Cunningham ran the drama club, so he couldn't be all that bad.

But he wasn't like Dr. Crowe. In the end, Mr. Cunningham was really no different from the other teachers. He thought Cole was a freak, too. It was easy to tell that. His eyes said it.

Today's lesson was on the front blackboard: *PHILADELPHIA — PLACE IN THE AMERICAN REVOLUTION.*

Cole rested his chin on his desk and cupped his arm around the perimeter. He blew a pencil across the surface until it reached his hand, then pushed the pencil back.

He'd read way past today's lesson in the textbook. He'd read all sorts of books on the history of Philadelphia. Seen things, too. He knew stuff about Philadelphia that Mr. Cunningham didn't know.

"Can anyone guess what city was the capital of the United States of America from 1790 to 1800?" Mr. Cunningham asked, gazing patiently around the classroom.

Not one person raised a hand.

"I'll give you a hint," the teacher went on. "It's the city you live in."

"Philadelphia!" the class sang out tepidly.

"Right," Mr. Cunningham said. "Philadelphia is one of the oldest cities in the country. A lot of generations have lived and died in this city. Almost every place you visit has a history and story behind it — even this school and the grounds they sit on. Can anyone guess what this building was used for a hundred years ago — before you went here, before *I* went to this school even?"

Cole raised his hand. If there was one place he knew especially well, it was this building. The rooms and hallways had secrets, bad secrets he wished he'd never learned. And not only the ones Mrs. Deems had told him.

"Yes, Cole?" Mr. Cunningham said.

"They used to hang people here," Cole replied.

Mr. Cunningham's face squinched up. "That's not correct. Where'd you hear that?"

"They'd pull the people in crying and kissing their families good-bye," Cole continued. "People watching would spit on them."

Now the kids were looking at each other. Rolling their eyes.

Well, it was the truth. Wasn't that what you were supposed to learn in school, the truth?

"Cole, this was a legal courthouse," Mr. Cunningham explained. "Laws were passed here. Some of the first laws of this country. This building was full of lawyers . . . lawmakers."

"They were the ones who hanged everybody," Cole said.

The Eye. Mr. Cunningham was giving him the Eye now. Cole hated that.

He turned away, staring at the floor.

"I don't know which one of these guys told you that," Mr. Cunningham said, gesturing around the classroom, "but they were just trying to scare you, I think."

Tommy Tammisimo started snickering. The giggles spread up and down the aisles until everybody — everybody — was laughing. They were *all* giving Cole the Eye. Even Bobby O'Donnell.

His skin crawled and his stomach turned and his face grew red.

The dark feeling was growing inside. The words would come next. The words and the shouting and the embarrassment and the detention and the calls home and —

"I don't like people looking at me like that!" Cole snapped.

"Like what?" Mr. Cunningham said.

He was still doing it — staring at Cole as if he were some strange life-form from another dimension. "Stop it!" Cole shouted.

Mr. Cunningham wouldn't stop. Mr. Perfect. He thought he was so perfect. A perfect haircut, perfect clothes, perfect everything. Well, he wasn't. *He wasn't.*

"I don't know how else to look —" Mr. Cunningham said. He was trying to sound patient. But Cole knew he was anything but.

The words exploded from Cole's mouth. "*You're a stuttering Stanley!*"

Mr. Cunningham's face fell. "Excuse me?"

"YOU TALKED FUNNY WHEN YOU WENT TO SCHOOL HERE. YOU TALKED FUNNY ALL THE WAY TO HIGH SCHOOL!"

The giggling stopped. Now they were all staring, totally silent. It was worse when they were silent. It meant they thought he was a . . . was a . . .

Mr. Cunningham stepped closer, his face turning red. "What —?"

"You shouldn't look at people!" Cole said. "It makes them feel bad."

"How did you —?"

"Stop looking at me!" Cole couldn't take any more. He put his hands over his eyes.

"Who have you been s-speaking to?"

There it was. The stutter. It was coming back. See, Stanley wasn't so perfect. He got nervous, too. He hated when people made *him* feel bad.

"STUTTERING STANLEY! STUTTERING STANLEY!" Cole cried.

"Who —?"

"STUTTERING STANLEY!"

"S-sss-stop it!"

He was right near Cole's desk now. *Why wasn't he going away?*

"STUTTERING —"

Mr. Cunningham slammed his fist on Cole's desk. Cole lurched back and dropped his hands from his eyes.

The teacher's face was inches away. He was bent over, the veins in his neck bulging and his eyes red as he blurted out, *"SHHHH-SHHHUT UP, YOU F-F-FFFFFREAK!"*

CHAPTER 8

Malcolm poked his head in the door of the St. Anthony's library. It was dark, stuffy, and brown — brown-stained wood, brown-leather chairs, brown-patterned Oriental rugs. It smelled of old leather and the dust accumulated on books that appeared to have been untouched for decades. It was the kind of place that made you feel very, very stupid.

Cole was nowhere to be seen.

As Malcolm turned to leave, he spotted a tiny movement — a hand flopping impatiently on the arm of a wide, high-backed chair.

The chair's back was to him. It faced a large mahogany librarian's desk.

Directly across it, the librarian's chair was empty.

They'd left Cole here all alone. Clearly the school had given up on him. Even the expensive private schools didn't have the resources to deal with a kid like Cole.

Nervous breakdown, Tourette's syndrome, attention deficit disorder — many diagnoses were on Cole's health report, but none of them seemed to hit the nail on the head.

If Cole was to stay at St. Anthony's, he would have to change. And his graduation was a big priority to Lynn Sear.

Graduation wasn't Malcolm's immediate concern, however. Cole's mental health came before everything. Understand the child, and the rest will follow.

"Hey, big guy," Malcolm said, sauntering around the desk.

Cole's eyes were flinty and red. He stared straight ahead, his lips tight and his shoulders stiff. He practically spat out his words. "I don't want to talk about anything."

Outside the windows, recess was in full swing. Malcolm sat in the librarian's chair, gazing at a game of tag that seemed to involve mandatory leaping into a pile of leaves. He smiled. The kids were squealing with laughter, oblivious to the condition of their nice school uniforms. Malcolm imagined Cole didn't join in many playground games. Which was a shame. The kid desperately needed an outlet, a social life. The bizarre, paranoid outbursts in class were serious. Malcolm had seen the signs before.

Time to bring down the heat a bit.

"Do you like magic?" Malcolm asked.

Cole clearly didn't care.

But Malcolm went on anyway. He pulled a penny from his pocket and held it out in his right hand. "Observe the penny closely."

He made a fist around the penny and a fist with his left hand, too. Then he shook both hands above his head, rotating his arms in a circle. "I do the magic shake . . . and suddenly the penny has magically traveled to my left hand."

Malcolm held up his left hand, his fingers still clenched. "But that's not the end of the trick. With another magic shake, the penny travels to my shirt pocket."

He thrust his arms outward and punched himself lightly in the chest, never opening his hands. "But that's *still* not the end. I do a final magic shake, and suddenly — the penny returns to the hand where it started from."

Holding out his right hand, he unfolded his fingers and revealing the penny that had been there the whole time.

"That isn't magic," Cole snapped.

Malcolm feigned surprise. "What?"

"You just kept the penny in that hand the whole time."

"Who, me?"

Cole glared at him. His voice was sharp and sarcastic. "I didn't know you were funny."

Malcolm's head pounded with every step toward home. For any other kid, he'd be closing in a diagnosis: acute anxiety disorder, most likely. He'd assure the parents it was a treatable condition and they certainly wouldn't have to pay Malcolm's high fees — he had personally trained many of the therapists at the local clinic, and he'd recommend the best. Meanwhile the child would be monitored for signs of possible paranoid schizophrenia (always remote) and sent to a psychiatrist for medication if need be. Another successful case for Dr. Malcolm Crowe, Philadelphia's son, the man with all the answers.

The books indicated this treatment. Common sense indicated it. By all rights, he should follow the precedent here.

And he knew that if he did, Cole would be off on a similar path to the one that had eventually led Vincent to Forty-seven Locust Street.

Training and logic were out the window in this case. For the first time in his career, Malcolm was at a loss.

He slumped up his stoop and into the house. The pile of mail on the table had grown. He reached down toward it, but stopped when a voice cried out from the living room, "Malcolm, sit your cute butt down here and listen up!"

Janice Robertson. Anna's best friend. What on earth was she doing here? She lived in San Francisco now.

Malcolm peeked into the room. Janice stared back at him — from a TV set, in a bridesmaid's gown. Anna was watching their wedding video. The image was grainier and jumpier and more badly composed than he'd remembered. But it didn't matter. The memories all rushed back in vivid detail.

Anna's blanket lay on the back of the sofa, and the remote rested on the arm. But the sofa itself was empty.

On the screen, Janice stood nervously before the reception tent, fumbling with a microphone — just as it was those years ago. In her pastel gown she looked a bit younger, a bit thinner, but it was hard to see her features for the streaks of black eyeshadow left by her tears.

Guests whirled on the dance floor behind her as she composed herself and spoke, in a voice choked with emotion: "No doubt about it, Anna's like my sister. She's got so much love for you, Malcolm. Don't tell her I told you, but she said she loved you from the first time she met you on the street. She'd do anything for you. . . . I love you guys. . . ." She began sobbing, sniffling back more tears and turning from the camera with embarrassment. "My nose is running. Why isn't someone getting me a tissue?"

Malcolm smiled.

The camera circled around Janice, zooming in on the dance floor, and suddenly the screen was filled with Malcolm and Anna, swaying in each other's arms, oblivious to everything else.

Oh, did he remember this. The air had a taste that day — cool and intoxicating, as if each breath both filled and expanded his deepest dreams. The band could have been playing in three different keys, but he and Anna wouldn't have noticed. They were reading each other's minds, communicating in smiles and movements, in secret shaded glances.

She'd do anything for you. Janice was right. In the years since the wedding, Anna had proven it a thousand times.

What had gone wrong?

Maybe she'd done one too many things without receiving what *she* needed. Maybe Malcolm simply didn't have the same capacity to love. He had it inside him, Lord knows. But clearly he hadn't shown it — or even told her. For all his work unlocking the complicated emotions of other people, Malcolm had always played his own cards close to the vest. Instead of saying "I love you," he joked.

And now he wanted so badly to tell her how he felt, to soothe her anger. But a line had been crossed. Somehow he'd blown it. His office was in the basement and maybe the time for a second chance had passed.

Why had Anna been playing this video — and why had she left in the middle of it? Maybe, he hoped, she was searching for a way to reignite her love for him.

Maybe she was just reminding herself of what she'd lost.

Malcolm headed into the bedroom. He heard the hiss of the shower and walked to the bathroom.

Anna was showering. She didn't see him; she was in her own world. The medicine cabinet hung ajar, and Malcolm spotted an unfamiliar bottle open on a shelf.

ANTI-DEPRESSANT, the label read. TO BE TAKEN TWICE DAILY.

Malcolm's heart sank. Anna *never* took medication. She didn't even like aspirin.

This was serious. And she hadn't told him — a *psychologist*, for pete's sake. Why?

It was all unraveling, wasn't it — his work, his marriage, his life.

The man with all the answers didn't understand a thing.

CHAPTER 9

"Then you do the magic shake . . ."

Cole whirled his fists in the air, clutching a penny in his right hand. Bobby O'Donnell stared at him dully.

They were the only two kids in Darren Winthrop's dining room. The rest had run into the living room to play with Darren's birthday presents. Wrapping paper, balsa-wood airplanes, a Nerf football, and several Lego pieces flew through the air, as the kids ran around their chatting parents who pretended not to mind the chaos.

"And now," Cole continued with a smile, "the penny moves from my pocket . . . all the way to the hand it started in!"

He dropped his hands to the table and unclenched his fists, revealing the penny.

"That's stupid," Bobby said.

Cole's smile disappeared. "It's supposed to be funny."

"It's stupid. I want my penny back."

Dejected, Cole shoved the penny across the table. Bobby took it and slid off his seat, headed for the kitchen.

Cole wandered toward the Winthrops' carpeted spiral stairway. Like everything in their house, it was enormous and plush and spotlessly clean. The Winthrops were new rich, as opposed to old rich — at least that was what Tommy said. Cole didn't know the difference, but it sure seemed to mean something to Tommy.

Mama was happy Darren had invited Cole to the party. She thought that meant Darren liked him. Cole hoped so. Darren wasn't too bad. He did admit that his dad had made him invite Cole — but Mama said to ignore that; he was probably lying, just showing off in front of the other kids.

Mama was talking with Mrs. Winthrop now. Their conversation drifted in from the living room.

"He doesn't get invited places," Mama was saying.

"It's our pleasure," Mrs. Winthrop replied.

"The last time was a Chuck E. Cheese party a few years ago. He hid in one of those purple tunnels and didn't come out."

"Chuckie who?"

"Cheese. It's . . . a kid's place."

Cole wondered what it was like to be rich. You probably had to do things that were pretty boring and gross. Darren's family probably went to restaurants with French names and ate snails and frogs, like in the movies. He'd have to ask Darren about that.

A red balloon floated past Cole and into the hallway, curling around him on a stream of air, then rising in a lazy arc up the center of the stairwell. Cole smiled. He wished he could do that, just float away.

The stairway rose three floors, and at the top was a crystal chandelier that threw pretty patterns of light on the walls. Cole walked up, entranced by the way the balloon danced in the reflections.

He could hear Darren and Tommy at the bottom of the stairs now. Tommy, as usual, was bragging about his TV commercial job. "I even got a trailer," he said.

"For what?" Darren asked. "You only had one line."

"You're slow, you know that?" Tommy shot back. "The star of the commercial always has his own trailer. You need to think about your character, alone."

But Cole wasn't paying them much attention. At the top of the first landing, a filigreed wrought-iron gate stood open. Behind it was a small, dark closet door.

Suddenly Cole felt very, very cold.

And he knew he wasn't alone.

"Open this door, please!" a muffled voice called from inside.

No, Cole thought. No. Not here.

Thump thump thump thump. "I can't breathe! Open this door, I didn't steal the master's horse. OPEN THIS DOOR OR I'LL BREAK THROUGH AND GRAB YOU!"

Cole jumped away. The door was on the verge of buckling outward.

"Hey, what's up?"

Cole spun around with a start. Darren and Tommy were climbing up the stairs.

"Happy birthday, Darren," Cole squeaked.

Tommy gestured to the closet door. "Something you want to see in there?"

"No!" Cole blurted out.

"We're going to put on a pretend play," Tommy said evenly. "You want to be in it?"

"Okay . . ." Cole answered tentatively.

"It's called, 'Locked in the Dungeon,'" Tommy explained.

"Yeah, Cole," Darren said, quickly adding, "you get to be the one locked in the dungeon!"

Cole didn't have time to react. The boys grabbed him by the arms and shoved him backward. Darren grabbed the closet doorknob and pulled the door open.

"Do-o-o-on't!" Cole screamed.

He kicked and flailed, but the boys threw him into the pitch-black closet and slammed the door shut.

Lynn heard it first. A scream audible, it seemed, only to her. The other mothers at the party chattered and went about their business. But Lynn knew. Despite the loud music she knew something was very wrong.

She was up the stairs in a nanosecond. Darren and Tommy were standing on a step, motionless like a couple of rag dolls. She swept past them and grabbed the closet door. "Cole! *COLE?*"

"STOP IT!" he was yelling. *"LEAVE ME ALONE! NO! NO-O-O-O-O!"*

It was locked tight. She yanked on the knob, twisted as hard as she could. She could feel the pounding through the door — savage, brutal. *"CO-O-O-O-OLE!"*

Lynn let go, paralyzed with panic. A few steps below, everyone stood and watched her. No one was climbing up to help. No one. They were killing him, she couldn't get in, and not one of them was lifting a finger —

A loud, sickening thud came from the closet, and Cole stopped screaming.

Lynn lunged at the door once again and pulled with all her strength.

This time it opened easily. Cole tumbled into her arms. He was limp, motionless, his neck and arms covered with scratches. She turned and carried him down the stairs, through the group of gaping, useless people.

Behind her, in the open closet, were two old storage chests.

Nothing else.

CHAPTER 10

Malcolm sat tensely in the reception area of the pediatric hospital. The seats were shorter than normal here, the table strewn with action figures, dolls, odd geometric games, and many dog-eared magazines.

Across the table, Lynn looked compressed and hopeless in her little seat. Malcolm felt for her. A house full of guests, and not one had offered to accompany her here. If he hadn't come to join her, she'd be all alone.

Dr. Hill, the young, sharp-eyed resident in charge of Cole, emerged from the hospital corridor. He sat opposite them and began opening a manila folder.

"What's wrong with Cole?" Lynn asked anxiously.

"The tests indicate he did not have a seizure," Dr. Hill replied. "In fact, he's doing fine. After some rest, he could go home tonight."

Lynn closed her eyes and exhaled a lungful of tension.

But Dr. Hill's words had been measured and flat, his expression far from encouraging. He was looking at Lynn with cool, appraising eyes.

Malcolm spotted a young woman with a clipboard and a professional smile standing in the doorway. "There's something else going on, Lynn," he said softly.

Lynn's eyes opened. She caught Dr. Hill's glance and sat up straight. He wanted to tell her something. "What is it?"

"There are some scratches and bruises on your son that concern me," the doctor said.

"Oh, man . . ." Malcolm groaned. Not this.

"Those are from sports, from playing," Lynn explained. "He's not the most coordinated kid, but I don't want him to stop trying — you know what I mean?"

"Mrs. Sloan over there is our social worker at the hospital," Dr. Hill said. "She's going to ask you some procedural questions."

Lynn's face darkened. She rose slowly from her chair. "You think I hurt my child? *You think I'm a bad mother?*"

"At this point it's just procedure," Dr. Hill said evenly. "And you should probably calm down."

Malcolm stood up. The young ones were the most heartless, the ones fresh out of school. They could rip out your soul and expect you to say thanks. "How do you *expect* her to react?" he asked.

"You want me to answer your questions?" Lynn said through clenched teeth.

"I'm sorry if I was being vague," Dr. Hill replied. "Yes, I do."

"Well, who's going to answer mine?" Lynn demanded. "What happened to my child today? Something was happening to him —*physically* happening. *Something was very wrong!*"

Dr. Hill snapped his folder shut, gestured toward Mrs. Sloan, and left the room.

Cole didn't look up as Malcolm entered the hospital room. The boy was curled up tight, his head resting on two hospital pillows, his hands clutching a light-purple blanket to his chin, as if to protect himself. He gazed listlessly out the window of his room, across an airshaft into the next wing of the building.

He had never seemed so small and vulnerable. Malcolm sat at the foot of the bed, wanting desperately to make everything all better.

Cole's foot stuck out from beneath the blanket. On it was a man's dress sock, hanging in folds like a sack.

Malcolm realized the father hadn't been contacted about this incident. There hadn't been enough time, with Lynn answering the social worker's questions and Malcolm helping out and planning his own strategies. But the father was an important factor in this case. Malcolm wondered how he had reacted to Cole's behavior as the boy was growing up. The report hadn't said much about Ken Sear. Only that the boy missed him and the mother didn't.

"Did your father ever tell you bedtime stories?" Malcolm asked.

Cole's voice sounded flat and distant. "Yes."

Maybe that would calm him down, make the hospital seem homier. Malcolm quickly improvised the beginning of a simple story and began reciting: "Once upon a time there was a prince, who was being driven around. They drove around for a long, long time. Driving . . . driving . . . driving a lot. They drove some more, and then he fell asleep. Then he woke up and saw they were still driving. It was a very long trip —"

"Dr. Crowe?" Cole interrupted.

"Yes?"

"You haven't told bedtime stories before."

Malcolm's face reddened. "No."

"You have to add some twists and stuff. Maybe they run out of gas."

"No gas . . . hey, that's good." Malcolm nodded his head. Twists. The father must have been a good yarn spinner. Perhaps this was one of the reasons for Cole's active imagination. So, say the car has no gas, then what?

"Tell me a story about why you're sad," Cole said.

Malcolm's thoughts screeched to a halt. "You think I'm sad? What makes you think that?"

"Your eyes told me."

"I'm not supposed to talk about stuff like that." As the words left his mouth, Malcolm realized how dumb they sounded. It was his standard response — all the books said that psychotherapists were supposed to keep their personal lives out of the professional relationship.

But if Malcolm were to get through, he

would have to take risks. He was already following the kid around now, inserting himself into every aspect of Cole's personal life. This had gone beyond a clinical relationship. Cole was curious. Why not let him know who Malcolm Crowe really was, let him see past the so-called expert to the human being underneath?

Cole was cocking his head, waiting for an answer.

Malcolm looked away, his thoughts racing back over the past year. "Once upon a time," he began, "there was a boy named Malcolm. He worked with children. Loved it more than anything. Then, one night, he finds out he made a mistake with one of them. Didn't help that one at all. He thinks about that one a lot. Can't forget."

A broken window. That was how it all started. A broken window and a broken young man. Then — what? A broken marriage. Two broken lives. And a trail of pieces to pick up.

"Ever since then," Malcolm continued, "things have been different. He's become messed up — confused, angry. Not the same person he used to be. His wife doesn't like the person he's become. They barely speak anymore. They're like strangers."

Malcolm felt his eyes moisten. Another broken rule — you never let the patient see your personal suffering.

He turned and met Cole's rapt gaze. "And then one day, this person Malcolm meets a wonderful boy who reminds him of that one. Reminds him a lot of that one. Malcolm decides to try to help this new boy. He thinks maybe if he can help this boy, it would be like helping that one, too."

Malcolm stopped. That was it. The whole story in a nutshell.

The ball was in Cole's court now.

"How does the story end?" the boy asked.

"I don't know . . ." Malcolm slowly shook his head. His words trailed off into a long, swollen silence.

"I want to tell you my secret now," Cole whispered.

Malcolm was jolted out of his haze. He hadn't expected this. "Okay."

Cole paused. His face was ashen. "I see people," he said, his voice a whisper. "I see dead people. Some of them scare me."

I see dead people . . .

"In your dreams?" Malcolm asked.

Cole shook his head no.

"When you're awake?"

Cole nodded.

"Dead people, like in graves and coffins?"

"No. Walking around, like regular people. They can't see each other. They only see what they want to see. They don't know they're dead."

"They don't know they're dead?"

"I see ghosts. They tell me stories — things that happened to them. Things that happened to people they know. They always want something from me."

Malcolm's mouth became suddenly dry.

Delusions. Voices. This was out of left field. Different than Vincent Gray. Vincent had never talked about ghosts.

"How often do you see them?" Malcolm asked, trying to keep his professional cool.

"All the time. They're *everywhere*." Cole's voice was barely audible now. "You won't tell anyone my secret, right?"

"No," Malcolm replied.

"Will you stay here till I fall asleep?"

Malcolm nodded. He sat rock-still as Cole pulled up in his blanket and turned on his side. At that moment, Malcolm didn't want to be alone either.

Sleep came quickly for the boy, and soon Malcolm left. He made his way quickly through the neon-washed corridors of the hospital, not saying a word until he was on the street.

At the corner he pulled out his pocket voice recorder and put it close to his mouth.

"Cole," he said under his breath. "His pathology is more severe than initially assessed. He's suffering from visual hallucinations, paranoia — symptoms of some kind of school-age schizophrenia. Medication and hospitalization may be required."

He pressed the off button, dropped the machine in his pocket, and muttered the words he didn't dare record:

"I'm not helping him."

CHAPTER 11

Lynn pushed the door open with her hip. She was carrying Cole on her shoulder, his red cotton sweater under his head as a pillow. This was a lot harder than it used to be when he was little, but she did it with grace and speed, slipping into the front hall and heading straight for his bedroom.

Mrs. Sloan hadn't been too harsh, thank goodness. She was a mother, too, and she recognized the agony that Lynn felt. By the end of the question-and-answer session, they were both crying.

Lynn had hoped she could take Cole away from the sterile hospital room early enough so that he could fall asleep in his own bed. But by the time she had completed the paperwork and gotten to his room, he was already snoring.

No matter. He'd wake up tomorrow to Mama and Pop-Tarts, home sweet home. No more hospital walls. No more having to face those horrible boys at their awful homes.

Sebastian was already snoozing on the bedspread, warming it up for Cole. Gently Lynn lay her son down next to the puppy and rested Cole's head on his pillow.

She took his red sweater from her shoulder and folded it neatly. Her finger slipped through a moth hole she wasn't aware of. Odd. The sweater was brand-new.

Holding it up to the lamp, she saw that it wasn't a moth hole at all. It was a rip. Parallel to it were two others, as if the sweater had been torn from Cole's neck by very strong fingers.

What on earth had happened to him on those stairs?

Her eyes focused on the back of Cole's T-shirt. It, too, was ripped in three places, corresponding exactly to the holes on the sweater.

She pulled back the shirt. Three long, deep scratches had gouged his skin diagonally across his left shoulder blade.

Finger marks. Through the sweater and shirt.

How vicious did a kid have to be to leave these — how full of hate and evil? Was this the reason they had invited her child to the party? To abuse him and lock him in a closet? To hospitalize the kid from the other side of the tracks? Did this make them feel better about themselves?

No way was she working two jobs — scrapping by on five hours' sleep a night — to send her son to a school where he was a target for spoiled, rich hoodlums.

Without waking Cole, she carefully removed his tattered shirt. She could see the hospital had treated the cut, but the bandage had fallen off. Quickly she retrieved one from the bathroom, applied it, and pulled the covers over her son.

Then she stormed into her bedroom and tapped out the Winthrops' phone number. At this hour, she'd wake someone, but she didn't care.

"Hello?" said a groggy voice.

"Hi, this is Lynn Sear, Cole's mother. I wonder if we could talk about your son and his goddamn friends keeping their hands off my boy?"

Cole's eyes opened. He was home. Mama had come and gotten him.

That was good, because he really had to go to the bathroom. He had held it in because he hated the hospital bathroom. He hated the hospital, period. There was no place to hide from *them*. They were all over the place. He could see them when he looked out the window, wandering the corridors in the hospital wing across the airshaft.

It was a good thing Dr. Crowe had visited. Otherwise he might not have fallen asleep.

He jumped off his bed and walked out the door. Quickly he checked the hallway, because you never knew.

Then, tiptoeing as fast as he could, he ran across the hall and did his business.

What a relief.

As he reached out to flush, he heard a movement.

Behind him. In the hallway.

He turned slowly. It was freezing cold, and he felt goose bumps on the flesh of his arms and scalp. As he leaned on the doorjamb, peering into the hallway, he could see his breath. That was a sign.

He eyed the red tent inside his bedroom door. The saints were in there, and Jesus and

Mary and all those other figures from church. He would be safe there. Safe from the dead people.

To his left, a shaft of light slanted across the carpet from the kitchen entrance. He heard the sound of oil popping on a skillet, vegetables being chopped.

Mama — at this hour?

Lately she'd been having insomnia. He and she had that in common. Sometimes they sat in the kitchen together and had hot cocoa. She didn't usually cook anything, though.

Cole crept toward the kitchen and looked in.

Her back was to him. She was wearing a bathrobe, leaning over the stove. All the kitchen cupboards and drawers were open.

"Mama?" he said. "Dream about Daddy again?"

She stiffened.

"DINNER'S NOT READY!"

As she whirled around, Cole lurched backward. It wasn't Mama at all.

She glared at him through bloodshot eyes, one of them black and blue. Her face was hideous, old and ugly and all scratched up. It was the lady who opened all the cabinets, the one who'd visited a few mornings ago, when Mama had seen the spot on his tie.

"What are you going to do?" she demanded, her voice harsh and sarcastic.

His heart pounding wildly, Cole stepped backward, toward the hallway.

"YOU CAN'T HURT ME ANYMORE!" With a demented grin, she thrust her arms forward, palms up.

Her wrists had been slashed open with a knife.

Cole nearly fell as he scrambled out of the kitchen. The tent. He had to get to the tent.

He ran into his bedroom and dived through the tent flap. His whole body shook. He pulled the flap closed, then snatched a flashlight off the floor and flicked it on.

The light, reflected off the sheets, cast the interior in a deep red. Beside him, lined up carefully on a wooden rack, were his figurines. They smiled down at him. Everything is all right, their faces said.

"De profundis clamo ad te Domine . . ." Cole began whispering.

CHAPTER 12

"Okay, kids, house lights to half . . ." Mr. Cunningham said in an excited whisper. "We've got a big crowd out there. Don't be nervous. House lights off . . . and *curtain*!"

Stacey Stratemeyer began yanking the curtain open. Cole peeked out from behind his body-size cardboard monkey cutout. The stage lights washed over the seats of the darkened St. Anthony's auditorium, reflecting against a sea of camcorder lenses.

He saw Dr. Crowe and Mama, both clapping and grinning proudly as they read the banner draped across the stage: THE THIRD AND FOURTH GRADE PRESENT — RUDYARD KIPLING'S THE JUNGLE BOOK.

"Break a leg, kids!" Mr. Cunningham called out, and he and nudged Tommy Tammisimo to the stage.

Tommy strutted out with a big, conceited grin. "There once was a boy," he exclaimed in a British accent, "very different from the other boys. He lived in the jungle and he could speak to the animals!"

That was Cole's cue. He crab-walked onto the stage along with all the other kids playing trees, native villagers, giraffes, tigers, and elephants.

It was a small part. But he knew he was the most convincing on the stage.

After the play, after Mama had kissed him and told him what a great actor he was before running off to her job, Cole took a long time getting ready to leave. He liked being on stage. It was a little like being in the tent, or in church. He felt safe, surrounded by light and good energy. He couldn't wait for "Young King Arthur," the drama club presentation later this month. Maybe he'd have a bigger role this time. At one time he'd wanted Mr. Cunningham to cast him as Galahad or Lionel or even Mordred — but after Cole's outburst in class, he was more likely to be a dragon or a horse. Or the stone embedded with the sword. Tommy would love that.

Dr. Crowe met him at the stage door and walked with him through the school. The corridors were empty now, and their footsteps echoed against the floor tiles.

"Did you think the play sucked big time?" Cole asked.

"What?" Dr. Crowe said.

"Tommy Tammisimo acted in a cough syrup commercial. He thought all of us were self-conscious and unrealistic. He said the play sucked big time."

"I know every child is special in his or her own way, but Tommy sounds like a punk," Dr. Crowe said. "I thought the play was excellent. Better than *Cats*."

"Cats?"

"Never mind."

Whatever. Cole couldn't help smiling. It was nice having Dr. Crowe on his side.

They took a left and walked silently toward the school's side exit, near the gym.

"Cole," Dr. Crowe said, "I was really interested in what you told me in the hospital. I'd like to hear more about it."

Cole had to think for a moment.

The ghosts — they had started talking about the ghosts. Why did Dr. Crowe want to talk about them *now*?

Cole didn't quite know how to tell Dr. Crowe about them. He'd have to be very careful.

As they passed a narrow stairway, Cole felt a chill.

They were here.

He froze, standing absolutely still. He heard the squeak of the dangling ropes, and he knew.

He had seen them before, in this same place. Right above those stairs was the chamber. The place where the people were punished.

He wished he and Dr. Crowe had gone out the front door, not here.

"What's wrong?" Dr. Crowe asked.

Cole tried not to look but he couldn't help it. There were three of them, a black family — man, woman, and boy. Runaway slaves, probably. They were barefooted and dressed in old raggedy clothes, hanging from the ropes used to strangle them to death. And they were staring.

Cole forced himself to look at the floor as he pointed up to the bodies.

Dr. Crowe turned to look. "Is something in there? What is it? I don't see."

"Be real still," Cole said. "Sometimes you feel

Cole Sear is haunted by a dark secret: He is visited by ghosts.

"I was thinking," Cole tells Dr. Malcolm Crowe, "you're nice. But you can't help me."

De profundis clamo ad te Domine. "Out of the depths, I cry to you, Lord" — Cole recites the mass for the dead with his toy soldiers.

"You know, you can tell me things if you need to." Lynn, Cole's mom, is desperate to find out what's tormenting him.

"Think about what you want from our time together," Malcolm tells Cole.
"Can it be something I don't want? I don't want to be scared anymore."

Magic tricks are an illusion —"but some magic's real," Cole knows.

Voices coming from the crawl space in the attic summon Cole.

it inside — like you're falling down real fast, but you're really just standing still. . . . Do you ever feel prickly things on the back of your neck?"

"Yes?" Dr. Crowe said.

"And the tiny hairs on your arm," Cole continued. "You know when they stand up?"

"Yes?"

"That's them. When they get mad, it gets cold."

Cole held tight, squeezing all his muscles. To keep away the cold. And the falling sensation. And the fear.

Cole hoped Dr. Crowe would be different — that he would see what Cole could see.

But just like the others, he couldn't see.

"I don't see anything," Dr. Crowe said, squinting anxiously at the landing, the ceiling, the shadows of the hallway.

The three bodies dangled heavily, their necks bent and broken, their eyes wide and buggy and staring straight ahead.

The eyes. Not the eyes.

"Please make them leave," Cole said.

Malcolm took his hand and shot a look back up the stairs. "I'm working on it."

CHAPTER 13

Lynn pulled a nice piece of juicy roast beef off the stove. She'd bought a big supply of meat during the sale at the A&P this week. Cole's color had been off lately, and the protein and iron would do him good.

His eyes were glued to a cartoon on the kitchen TV. As she served him his meal, he barely noticed. That was okay. At least he was smiling. She was grateful for that. He was always easier to talk to when he was in a good mood.

And she had some serious things to talk to him about.

It was suddenly very chilly in here. As Lynn

returned to the stove for her own plate, she detoured to the thermostat and turned it way up. "I don't care what they say," she murmured. "This thing is broken."

A familiar tinny, high-pitched voice cried out from the TV: "Mommeeeee, my throat hurts!"

Tommy Tammisimo. In full color. Standing in bedroom doorway, dressed in pj's. Again. They played that darn commercial all night long. She and Cole had seen it a million times.

On the screen, the actors who played the perfect parents exchanged a knowing glance, not a hair out of place as they left their bed, took Tommy to the bathroom, fed him cough syrup . . . and now the syrupy music . . . here comes the friendly announcer. . . .

"Pedia-ease Cough Suppressant," a deep voice intoned. "Gentle, fast, effective."

Miraculous was more like it. Cut to Mr. and Mrs. Yuppie the next morning, looking out their spotless window as a now-cured Tommy frolics in the yard with his dog. He waves ecstatically, they wave back. . . .

Cole threw a shoe at the screen. The TV lurched backward, the plug yanked out of its socket, and the image went blank.

Lynn didn't like him throwing things. Violence was not the answer. But she let this one go. Tommy deserved it.

She did mind, however, that Cole was wearing his father's winter gloves while he tried to drink his milk. Her ex-husband had been in such a hurry to leave, he hadn't had the decency to remove all his possessions and spare her the grim reminders. Now Cole insisted on wearing his stuff all the time. "Take 'em off," she said.

Cole obediently removed the gloves and placed them next to his milk glass.

"I don't want them on my table," Lynn snapped.

As Cole put them on the floor, Lynn pulled out a chair and sat opposite him. They ate in silence for a moment as she composed mentally what she needed to say. He had been taking things from her bedroom lately, and it had to stop.

She knew he had been sneaking religious figures from the church. She'd talked to Father Manahan about it, and he'd asked in a tactful way if Cole had ever shoplifted. When Lynn told him no, he'd smiled and said not to worry. Cole was a good boy and he clearly needed the comfort of the saints. When he was older, his conscience would lead him to confess, and he would return the figures. The church, of course, would be there for him with forgiveness. Let the church be there for him now.

But now he'd been using his sticky fingers at home. And that was just plain wrong.

"I saw what was in your bureau drawer when I was cleaning," she said, trying to keep the accusation out of her voice.

Cole glanced up from his plate. He looked worried.

"You got something you want to confess?" she asked.

Nothing. Not a word.

"The bumble bee pendant," she reminded him. "Why do you keep taking it?"

Now he was looking at his lap, about as guilty as a fox fleeing a chicken coop. She hated to see him like this. All he needed to do was tell her.

"It was Grandma's," Lynn said quietly. "What if it broke? You know how sad I'd be." It was one of the few precious things she had of her mother's. Even her memories were beginning to fade.

"You'd cry," Cole replied, "'cause you miss Grandma so much."

Lynn nodded. "That's right."

"Sometimes people think they lose things, and they really didn't lose them. It just gets moved."

Lynn gave him a puzzled look. "Did you move the bumble bee pendant?"

Cole shook his head silently.

Lynn tried to keep her cool. She couldn't understand him. When he got like this, he was on another planet.

"Don't get mad," Cole said.

"So who moved it this time?" Lynn demanded. "Maybe someone came into our house, took the bumble bee pendant out of my closet, and then laid it nicely in your drawer?"

"Maybe."

She was starting to see black. She wanted to pick him up, turn him upside down and shake this strange behavior out of his soul. But when she looked in his eyes, she saw the pain behind them—*felt* it, deeply—and she understood that anger was the last thing he needed.

He was a kid. He didn't know why he said and did things. He didn't know why other kids did things to him. He was confused. Lynn understood that.

But she was confused, too. And she fought

the questions that scorched the back of her brain: who understood *her*? Who looked into *her* eyes and knew the right things to say and do? She didn't need a therapist, she didn't need medication, she couldn't afford them anyway — but it wouldn't hurt to have a little rest, and just a *clue* about what was going on in her son's beautiful little head.

"I'm so tired, Cole," she pleaded. "I'm tired in my body. I'm tired in my mind. I'm tired in my heart. I need some help. I don't know if you noticed, but our little family isn't doing so good. I'm praying for us, but I must not be praying right. It looks like we're just going to have to answer each other's prayers. If we can't talk to each other, we're not going to make it."

She leaned in and searched Cole's dark eyes. "Now, baby, tell me. I won't be mad, honey. Did you take the bumble bee pendant?"

Cole tightened up. "No."

Lynn sat straight back and threw her napkin on her plate. That was it. She'd reached the end of her patience. "You've had enough roast beef. You need to leave the table."

He was hurt. His eyes were searching her, looking for — what? What did he want?

"Go!" she blurted out.

Pushing his seat back from the table, Cole stood on his little feet and walked to his room.

Cole hated when Mama got so mad. She was in the kitchen now, sniffling. Why did she care so much about the pendant? Why did she have to ask those questions?

He walked slowly down the hallway to his bedroom, wondering what he could have done differently, so she wouldn't get mad. He'd tried to keep silent about the pendant. It wasn't a sin to keep silent. But she'd forced him to speak up, so what else could he do?

He couldn't lie — *that* was a sin. So he'd told the truth. Just not all of it. That was the problem. He couldn't tell Mama who really moved the pendant. He couldn't tell her about the dead people. She definitely wouldn't be able to handle it. Just look at how she acted at the dinner table when he gave her a hint.

The only person he could tell was Dr. Crowe. Dr. Crowe was different, of course. He was used to hearing strange things from kids. That was his profession. And he wouldn't tell anyone Cole's secret.

But even Dr. Crowe didn't believe it.

As Cole walked down the hall to his bedroom, he heard Sebastian growl. An instant later the puppy scurried out of the room and raced past him into the kitchen.

Cole stopped.

Slowly, his door began to swing open.

A dark figure slipped out of the spare room and into the hallway. It glided swiftly into Cole's bedroom before he could see it clearly.

"Come on!" a voice called.

Cole's knees locked. A boy was leaning out of his doorway now, maybe thirteen or fourteen. "I'll show you where my dad keeps his gun," the boy said. "Come on!"

The boy turned to walk back in, and Cole saw the back of his head — or the lack of it. It had been blown off, leaving a dark, bloodied crater.

Cole shot back to the kitchen, his feet barely touching the floor.

Mama was on her knees, trying to convince Sebastian to come out from the broom closet. "Mama?" he said.

She turned, startled. Her eyes were red from crying, and she quickly wiped them. She didn't like to cry in front of Cole.

"If you're not very mad," Cole said, "can I sleep in your room tonight?"

"Look at my face, Cole," she said, a smile slowly softening her tear-stained face. "I'm not very mad."

Cole threw his arms around her and clenched her as tight as he could.

"Baby?" she said. "Why are you shaking?"

No. He couldn't tell. And he couldn't lie.

"Cole, what's *wrong?*" Mama pleaded, rocking him back and forth. "Please tell me. *Please* . . ."

She was crying again, but Cole just held her tight and felt her warmth, her comfort, until the fear started to go away.

CHAPTER 14

Anna Crowe loved when young engaged couples came into the shop. They made her think of the early days with Malcolm, when they'd go from store to store and say, *I want one of these, and one of these, and three of those . . . to go, please* — a chant only Malcolm could dream up. They only said it to each other, of course. In those days they had no money, just dreams.

This couple seemed interested in everything. The young woman was stunning, with raven hair and deep brown skin. She was well off, possibly a daughter of foreign royalty. Anna always knew — the tasteful tailored clothing, the lilt of speech, the easy body language around objects of great value. The man had wavy, dark hair and deep sensitive eyes. He seemed a bit more intimidated — a medical school student, perhaps, or a graduate fellow in classics.

One thing was unmistakable. They were in love. It changed the whole atmosphere of the store. Their feeling for each other was like a diaphanous covering that followed and protected them.

Anna had known that feeling well.

She missed it deeply. She missed it every day. But she knew the feeling came only once. When it was gone, you never got it back. And it *was* gone, no matter how hard she tried to rescue it from videos and memories.

Dear, sweet Sean thought he could waken it in her. He didn't really know about Malcolm, didn't know that he was still a part of her life. As hard as she tried to break away — moving his office to the basement, leaving his mail on the foyer table — she simply couldn't. Not yet. Not all the way. Somehow she needed him still. No matter what happened to her, a part of him would always remain.

Meanwhile she'd enjoy the feeling of love vicariously, through the visitors to her shop.

The young woman had already discovered the antique diamond engagement ring at the back of the store. Sooner or later everyone did. It had the most exquisite fire, a nearly perfect stone.

"It's Edwardian," Anna explained. "Beautifully worked. Entirely platinum with a mine-cut diamond and an actual color Burmese sapphire. It's timeless."

The young man attempted a casual smile. "Do you have anything . . . a little plainer?"

"Plainer?" His fiancée shot him a look. "You want a plain ring to go with your plain fiancée, is that how it is?"

"No, no! It's just — you're so beautiful —" The wheels were turning fast. "You're like a Burmese sapphire all by yourself. You don't *need* all that."

The young woman raised a skeptical eyebrow. "Uh-huh."

Anna unlocked the glass jewelry cabinet and took out the ring. "Why don't you two hold it?"

She placed the ring in the cupped hands of the couple. The fiancée was nearly breathless. The young man grimaced.

"Do you feel longing?" Anna asked.

"Excuse me?" the young woman said.

"When I touch this piece," Anna explained, "I feel a longing. I imagine the woman who owned this loved a man deeply she couldn't be with."

The young woman cast a knowing glance at Anna. "Did he have wavy hair and chestnut eyes?"

Her future husband looked suddenly perplexed.

"I don't know . . . but maybe," Anna said playfully. "A lot of pieces in this store give me feelings. I think maybe when people own things and then they pass away, a part of themselves gets printed on those things — like fingerprints."

Now both of them were gazing at her silently, reverently, as if she had just led them to the source of the world's ancient love secrets.

They both reached down and touched the ring, as if hoping those secrets would rub off.

In minutes, Anna was walking to the back of the shop to fill out the paperwork for the sale.

Sean had been out buying and was loading in a piece in through the side entrance. He had a lot of company loyalty for someone celebrating his twenty-seventh birthday, Anna thought. She was impressed he hadn't taken the day off, even though she'd offered it to him. The least she could do was get him a little something for the occasion. He loved F. Scott Fitzgerald, and the antiquarian bookseller on Broad Street happened to have a copy of *The Great Gatsby*, which he let Anna have in exchange for a set of bronze candlesticks.

She had left the book, wrapped, on his desk.

"You don't need someone with a Master's degree," Sean remarked, setting down a stout wooden bench. "You need a wrestler guy whose neck is larger than his head."

Anna laughed. "I need a wrestler with a Master's."

"What's this?"

Anna looked up from her papers. Sean had seen the gift and was examining it curiously.

"From you?" he asked.

Anna nodded.

"Is it wrestling tights?" He tore open the wrapper with a goofy, childlike grin and stared open-mouthed at the book.

"It's a first edition," Anna said.

"Wow, this is too much," Sean exclaimed. "It's perfect, Anna."

He pulled her up from her seat and embraced her. He was like a happy little puppy; if he'd had a tail, it would be sweeping the papers off her desk. She liked Sean. He was a good kid. Overeager sometimes, a little awkward, but in a way, those were his most endearing qualities.

She drew back a bit and returned his smile. But he didn't let go. He kept his arms around her waist, looking at her with his giant, blue-gray eyes.

Anna felt the eyes of the young couple on her. She knew she needed to complete the sale before they changed their minds — but she didn't move. She was surprised at the way this felt. Sean's arms cradled her just the right way. He was stronger than she would have expected, but he knew how to hold a woman with tenderness and grace, like a dancer. She loved the feeling. She hadn't felt anything as delicious in a long, long time.

So when he brought his fingers up to her face and lightly ran them down her cheek, she tried not to think of Malcolm at all. And when he brought his lips closer, she closed her eyes and hoped the young couple would understand.

SMMMMMMACKK!

The front door slammed, forcing Sean and Anna to leap back.

Shattered glass spilled over the welcome mat as the rolled-up blinds clattered and fell open.

Anna and Sean sprinted to the door and pulled it open. They looked to the right, up the street toward the river.

To the left, Malcolm strode away, weaving among the crowd.

CHAPTER 15

The pumpkin was huge. Much bigger than last year's Halloween pumpkin. It was wedged in with the rest of the groceries in the shopping cart — as was Cole.

He still loved to be pushed through the parking lot. He was a little old for it, and way too heavy, but Lynn didn't mind at all. It was one of the few carefree, childlike things Cole allowed himself.

The breeze was especially crisp today, and the flame-colored tree canopies seemed to radiate their own light against the cloudy sky. Days like this made Lynn want to rise up and soar over the earth. She hoped Cole felt it, too — but when she leaned over to look at him, she could see his mind was far away.

Lynn began veering left and right. She circled around to an open part of the lot, picking up speed.

Cole's hair began to blow back in the wind. He looked up to the sun, throwing his arms outward like the wings of an airplane.

Lynn whooped with joy, pushing harder, running.

She pulled up to the rear bumper of her old Volvo station wagon with a perfect landing. Cole lowered his arms.

He was smiling now.

Sometimes, Lynn knew, the simple joys were the best.

Simple joys. Simple hopes.

It was ironic, Malcolm thought. Today Cole wanted to talk. Today, for the first time, he sat on the floor by the coffee table and faced Malcolm eye-to-eye.

Today Malcolm was the frightened and confused one.

The scene from the antique shop looped endlessly in his head. It was like a bad soap opera. And it happened in front of the watching customers — in front of Malcolm, for pete's sake! Clearly Anna hadn't known he was there. But people in this neighborhood *knew* Malcolm. Did she think he wouldn't find out? Did she care?

Not enough. That was the problem. A bigger problem than any he'd ever faced. One that needed his full-time attention.

"You don't want to ask me questions today?" Cole asked.

Malcolm shook his head.

"Can I ask you then?"

"Yes," Malcolm said absently.

"What do you want, more than anything?"

Malcolm knew this stage of the therapeutic process. Role reversal. A healthy development. The patient, in effect, becomes the therapist and in doing so begins to project his own conflicts on the real therapist, thereby objectifying them and allowing an internalization of —

Stop.

No more jargon.

"I don't know," he replied.

"I told you what I want," Cole said.

"I don't know, Cole."

Cole nodded sagely. "Why don't you think about it for awhile?"

The boy was smart. He was asking the questions Malcolm had been trained to ask. This was a basic one. You had to teach patients to think for themselves. Only then could they see their goals and chart a path through their fears.

Malcolm thought about it.

"I know what I want," he said finally. "My goal is to speak to my wife — the way she and I used to speak, like there was no one in the world but us."

"How are you going to do that?" Cole asked.

Malcolm fought back the rush of blood to his face, the moisture that suddenly clouded his vision. He had planned to work up to this, but the boy had forced his hand.

"I can't be your doctor anymore," Malcolm said. "I haven't given my family enough attention. Bad things happen when you do that. Do you understand?"

Cole didn't reply for a long time. "Do you want to go home?" he said quietly.

"I have to," Malcolm answered.

"When?"

"Soon. One week. I'm going to transfer you. I know two psychologists who are exceptional —"

"Don't fail me."

"What?"

The words were like knives.

You failed me. That was the last thing Vincent had said, before he . . .

"Don't give up," Cole pleaded. "You're the only one who can help me. I know it."

He's a different kid than Vincent, Malcolm thought. There were coincidences, yes. But there were coincidences in all cases. Don't dwell on it. "Someone else can help you," he said. "Someone else can make you happy."

Cole was crying now. His pinched little face was red and he looked as if his entire world were crumbling.

"Dr. Crowe?" he whispered.

"Yes?"

"You believe me, right?"

Honesty, Malcolm thought.

"Dr. Crowe, you believe my secret, right?" Cole pressed on.

Only honesty.

"I don't know how to answer that," Malcolm said, turning away to avoid the boy's eyes.

"How can you help me," Cole said, "if you don't believe me?"

The question hung over him, as sudden and dark as a solar eclipse.

It was a question he'd faced without an adequate answer for years. How did a grown man sit and listen to hours and weeks and years of fantasy and fear? How did a man coax an unformed mind into reality without destroying its capacity to dream? How indeed?

He had no idea.

Cole reached into his pocket. He took out a penny and slid it across the table.

Malcolm looked curiously into the boy's bloodshot eyes.

"Some magic," Cole whispered, "is real."

CHAPTER 16

Sitting in his basement office late that afternoon, Malcolm gazed blankly at his fancy framed certificate from the city of Philadelphia. It was coated with dust now, wedged between two packing boxes.

Anna was still at work. Malcolm had thought about returning to the shop, but he was afraid of what he might do. Sean would be there, and so would plenty of customers. The temptation to cause a scene would be too strong. Better to wait until Anna came home.

His eyes wandered across the accumulated detritus of fifteen years' hard work.

They stopped at a box marked SESSION TAPES — VINCENT GRAY.

Malcolm leaned forward and pulled the box from its pile. He chose one at random, marked 7/1.

He popped it into the tape machine and pressed play.

He heard background static. A door closing.

"Sorry about that. Hope I didn't leave you alone too long." His own voice, nine years younger. *"Wow, it's cold in here."*

The scrape of a chair on a wooden floor. The old wooden office chair.

"Vincent, why are you crying?"

Malcolm remembered this now. He'd left to take a phone call that day. He'd only been gone a minute, but when he returned, Vincent was in tears. Shaking.

"Vincent?"

"Yes?"

The sound of the boy's voice astonished him. It was so much like Cole's. Timid, obedient. Wanting to say the right thing.

"What happened?" came Malcolm's question. *"Did something upset you?"*

Vincent sniffled. *"You won't believe."*

"I won't believe what?"

"I don't want to talk anymore. I want to go home now, okay? I want to go home."

"Okay, Vincent, you can go home."

End of session. The tape went silent.

Malcolm sat for a moment. Something had happened to Vincent while he'd been gone, some traumatic psychological experience—a daydream, a hallucination.

Or was it?

Malcolm rewound the tape.

"—about that. Hope I didn't leave you alone too long. Wow, it's cold in here—"

He rewound some more and caught his own voice again, earlier in the session.

"—like needles, either. When I was a kid, I had this blood test done—I threw up chili cheese fries all over this male nurse."

He heard Vincent's quiet chuckle in the background, then the opening of the office door.

"Excuse me," chirped the voice of his secretary, Linda, *"Doctor Reed is on line two."*

"Vincent, I have to take it," Malcolm heard himself saying. *"Give me a minute."*

"Okay."

Malcolm's and Linda's footsteps. Silence again.

Then, a sudden screech. A chair scraping the floor.

Malcolm jacked up the volume from 3 to 7.

He could hear Vincent's breaths now, quick and uneven. A panic reaction. Higher pitched than the rhythmic hissing of the cassette-tape static.

Something was wrong. Something about that hissing.

Malcolm stopped the tape, rewound it just a bit, and pressed play.

This time he slid the volume knob to 10. As high as it went.

The sound filled the basement as a whispered voice emerged from the static. Malcolm strained to make out the words.

"*—familia . . . no dejen que esto me pase . . . mi familia . . . yo no quiero morir . . . familia . . .*"

Malcolm's high school Spanish came back to him. *Don't let this happen to me*, the voice was saying. *My family . . . I don't want to die. . . .*

It wasn't Vincent's voice speaking.

Whose was it?

CHAPTER 17

Cole stood Private Jenkins on the railing of the church balcony. Jenkins was alone on the hilltop now, exposed to possible fire from the Laotian jungle commandos.

He stood Private Kinney next to him. Private Kinney was thinking about his wife. He didn't know she had a brain aneurysm, whatever that was. If he did know, he would be more careful, so he could get home and take care of her. He'd make sure to send her right away to Walter Reed Army Hospital.

Cole didn't know where the hospital was, but Kinney did. He talked about it a lot. Both

Kinney and Jenkins had visited him. They didn't look as good as the toy soldiers did. They were all burned and you could barely recognize their faces. Napalm was some sick stuff.

At the sound of rushing footsteps in the church, Cole glanced down. Dr. Crowe had run in. He was panting.

Weird. Cole had never seen him all out of breath like this; he was always so cool.

"Hello, again," Cole called out. "You want to be a lance corporal in Company M, Third Battalion, Seventh Marines? We're being dispatched to the Quang Nam province."

Dr. Crowe looked up. "Maybe later," he said.

Suddenly, Cole got it.

"Something happened, didn't it?"

"Yes, it did."

"Are you wigging out?"

"Yes, I am." Dr. Crowe glanced nervously around the empty church, then turned back to Cole. "Maybe these people — the people that died and are still hanging around — maybe they weren't ready to go. Maybe they wake up that morning, thinking they have a thousand things to do and a thousand days left to do them in, and then all of a sudden it's all taken away."

Cole lined up the rest of Company M on the floor. He hadn't expected to hear this and he didn't know what to say.

Just a few hours ago, Dr. Crowe hadn't believed. Now he sounded different — more like the way he used to sound, only better. Maybe this was part of the therapy. Maybe, in this last week, he was just going to play pretend or something.

"Do you know what *'Yo no quiero morir'* means?" Dr. Crowe asked.

It sounded a little like Latin, but different. Cole shook his head.

"It's Spanish," Dr. Crowe explained. "It means, 'I don't want to die.' What do those ghosts want when they talk to you? I want you to think about it really carefully, Cole."

Standing up slowly, Cole looked over the railing. "Just . . . help."

"Yes, I think that's right! I think they all want that. Even the scary ones."

Cole looked at Dr. Crowe steadily. He knew Dr. Crowe well now. Cole could tell when he was hiding things, when he was treating Cole like a kid. Dr. Crowe's eyes told everything. They would narrow and look away. Then there would be a joke.

But the eyes didn't waver a bit. Dr. Crowe's

expression held no hint of any joke. "You believe now?" Cole asked.

"I believe both of you now," Dr. Crowe said firmly, remembering he had told Cole about Vincent in the hospital. "And I think I might know how to make them go away."

"You do?"

"I think they know you're one of those very rare people that can see them. You need to help them."

"How?"

"Listen to them," Dr. Crowe said. "Everyone wants to be heard. Everyone."

Now Cole *knew* Dr. Crowe was wigging out.

Cole fiddled with Private Kinney. Private Kinney always screamed and yelled. He was scary and strong and bloody. So was the cabinet lady and the kid with the gun and so many of them.

Help them? No way.

"What if they don't want the help?" Cole asked. "What if they're just angry and they want to hurt somebody?"

"I don't think that's the way it works, Cole."

"How do you know for sure?"

Dr. Crowe was looking at Cole's arm now. At the cuts that were starting to heal.

"I don't," he said softly.

* * *

The sun was setting as Malcolm walked home. He had been thinking on his feet at the church. If he'd planned out his speech to Cole in advance, he never would have said a thing. It was crazy. Outrageous. If the board ever found out about this, they'd throw his license away and try to commit him to an institution.

But he had never been more certain of a course of treatment in his life.

As he turned up Locust Street, his heart suddenly quickened.

Sean was walking out of his front door. His *front door*, in full view of Malcolm's neighbors and friends. Who did this kid think he was?

They would have to have a talk. Right now.

Malcolm picked up the pace. Sean was climbing into his car.

"Hey!" Malcolm cried out.

As he reached the car, Sean turned on the ignition and sped away.

CHAPTER 18

Cole slept snuggled up to Sebastian that night, on the floor of his tent. He was awakened by a moan.

His eyes blinked open.

"Cole . . ." Mama's voice cried out from down the hall. "Cole, what's happening?"

He rushed out of the tent and ran to her bedroom. He paused at the open door, peering in. The sewing machine was still standing in the corner, the closet door was closed, the carpet was neat. No one had broken or upturned anything. *They* hadn't been here.

"Cole . . . what's happening to you?" Mama's eyes were closed. She was lying on her back, twisting and turning. "Is someone hurting you? I'll beat their asses."

She was only having a dream. False alarm.

Cole looked closely at Mama's face. It was all tight and lined, the way she got when she was really scared. She was seeing something. Something that made her feel bad.

Mama tried to be sweet and cheerful every day, but Cole knew how worried she was. It wasn't just the bumble bee pendant. She was worried he would never get better.

He stepped into the room and moved to her side. Softly he touched the side of her face.

"Mama, you sleep now," he whispered.

Mama's twisting eased. She smiled faintly, and her body grew still.

As her breathing became steady and deep, Cole slowly backed out of the room. He shut the door quietly and turned back toward his room.

His exhalation made a cloud of white vapor in the air.

He went rigid. It was freezing in the hallway.

The tent. He had to get to the tent.

He forced himself forward, scrambling into his room and through the bedsheet flap. Fumbling in the darkness, he found his flashlight and turned it on.

Above him, a clothesline snapped. And another.

He shone the light upward. The tent was coming apart.

Cole beamed the light at his figurines, but they weren't there.

A girl was. A pale, hollow-eyed girl about ten years old, wearing a flannel nightgown.

She opened her mouth to speak, and a cascade of vomit spilled out onto the floor.

"I'm feeling much better now," she said, reaching out to him.

Cole dropped the light. He bolted out of the tent. His foot caught the tent flap and pulled the whole thing off its supports. Frantically he shook himself loose, ran down the hallway, and flew under the living room sofa. Sebastian was already there, cowering.

Cole held his breath and waited for a noise — footsteps, a voice — but the house was silent, save for Sebastian's faint whimpering.

The tent was supposed to be safe. How did she get in? What did she want?

Cole didn't want to find out. She grossed him out. He would stay there until she was gone.

He wished Dr. Crowe were here right now.

He wished Dr. Crowe could know what this felt like.

What would *he* do? Try to help the girl? Talk to her while she puked?

Or would he be here under the couch, too?

Dr. Crowe was supposed to give Cole new ideas. To help him deal with his problem. But what if his ideas were wrong?

What Dr. Crowe wanted Cole to do was impossible. It was against all instinct. And instinct was what protected you. That's what Cole had learned in science — fear made you become like an animal, so you could jump out of harm's way without thinking. The way Sebastian had.

What would Dr. Crowe say to that?

Probably he would say humans were different than animals. He would say that sometimes you had to act against your instincts.

That was the point of what he'd said in church.

Cole felt his breathing even out. He thought about Dr. Crowe's advice.

Cole had been using his instincts all his life. Running from the ghosts. Hiding. But they always came back.

And they always kept asking the same things, over and over.

Listen to them, Dr. Crowe had said. *Everyone wants to be heard*.

The girl was a new one. But she'd be back, too. Night after night of hurling chunks onto his tent floor.

He couldn't take that.

Cole swallowed hard. He shimmied himself out from under the sofa and stood up.

Silently he entered the hallway.

A soft red glow came from his bedroom. The flashlight was still on under his fallen tent. He could see the outline of the girl, still sitting up, her head and shoulders now propping up the bedsheet.

Instinct.

Every muscle and nerve in his body wanted to turn back. But he fought the urge and forced himself forward.

Cole reached out to the tent and pulled the sheet away.

The girl looked up at him. Cole could see intravenous tubes hanging from her wrists. Once again vomit poured from her mouth, but he held his ground.

"I'm feeling much better," she repeated.

Cole's stomach turned. He breathed deeply, trying not to be nauseated.

The spit-up wasn't real, he told himself. She was dead.

She needed to be heard.

Counting to three to calm his nerves, he whispered, "Do you want to tell me something?"

The bus ride was taking forever. Cole didn't even know Philadelphia had so many neighborhoods. His black suit was scratchy and hot, his dress shoes were too tight, the seat was hard, and the morning sun was beating on his face and making him feel carsick.

Dr. Crowe didn't seem to mind. Grown-ups were used to being bored and uncomfortable.

Kyra Collins, the sick girl in the tent, had told Cole to go to her house, to her room. She'd told him to find an unlabeled videocassette and show it to her father. She'd given him an address and Cole had carefully written it down. Before he could ask her any further questions, such as how exactly she had died, she'd vanished.

Now the bus was leaving the city limits. Cole could tell, because the tall buildings were gone and the houses weren't attached.

"She came a long way to visit me, didn't she?" Cole asked.

"I guess she did," Dr. Crowe replied.

It was nearly afternoon by the time they reached their stop, in a quiet neighborhood with curving streets, lots of trees, and nicely kept lawns.

The bus driver pointed out where Kyra's street was. Finding the address was easy. Lots of cars were pulling up in front of a neat, shingled house in the middle of the block. People streamed across the lawn, heading for the front door.

By the curb, a woman was being held up by two men. She was crying so hard she could barely stand up. "Can someone get a glass of water?" one of the men called out.

Kyra sure had a big family. Or lots of friends. Or both.

Cole and Dr. Crowe followed the crowd. On the front lawn of the house, a little girl in a dark dress sat on a swing. She was blond, maybe four years old or so, and Cole knew by her face that she was Kyra's sister.

The swing was still. The girl wasn't even trying to move, just staring straight ahead as everyone walked past.

Cole wanted to talk to her. She looked so sad and lonely. But Dr. Crowe was walking ahead, up the front steps, so he followed behind.

In the living room, people cried and hugged and ate food from big platters. The house wasn't as fancy as Darren's, Cole thought, but it was nice. Everything was blue — blue-patterned wallpaper, blue carpets and furniture.

Hanging on the living room wall was a large painting of the Collins family. Kyra was smiling. She looked tanned and healthy, and so did her baby sister. Kyra's mom was blond and very pretty, and her dad had thinning hair and a kind face.

As Cole and Dr. Crowe wound their way through the guests, Cole heard fragments of conversation. He quickly learned some things that Kyra hadn't told him:

She had been bedridden for two years before she died.

She had seen six doctors, and none of them knew what was wrong.

Her little sister was falling ill now, with the same symptoms.

"God help them," Cole heard a man say.

When they reached the back of the living room, Cole and Dr. Crowe quietly slipped up a carpeted staircase.

The hallway at the top was narrow and quiet. A spindly I.V. apparatus stood near a door on the right, along with a stack of boxes labeled HOSPITAL SUPPLIES and MEDICAL WASTE — TOXIC.

The door was shut tight.

Cole suddenly felt chilly. And scared.

He glanced at a world map that hung on the hallway wall and imagined all the places he could escape to. "I wish I were somewhere else."

Dr. Crowe looked sympathetic. "Where will you go where no one has died?"

Good question, Cole thought. Antarctica, maybe, but you couldn't live there. "Don't go home, okay?" he said.

"I definitely won't," Dr. Crowe replied.

Cole turned the knob and pushed the door open. Kyra's room was stuffy, and it smelled like baby powder. The walls were full of colorful get-well cards and drawings. Her bed was a hospital bed, with a hand crank and a slanted mattress. Its sheets were still wrinkled, as if Kyra had gotten up for a stroll and was about to return.

But what really got Cole's attention were the puppets. Kyra's shelves were full of them — marionettes, finger puppets, Punch and Judy figures, witches and monsters, princesses and kings and queens. A small, three-sided puppet stage stood on her dresser, next to a small camcorder.

Kyra had told Cole to give one of the finger puppets to her sister, a clown with a pointed hat. He found it, put it in his pocket, and moved on.

On Kyra's desk, videocassettes had been lined in neat rows. Cole examined them carefully. CHRISTMAS SHOW, one label said. PUPPET SHOW CLASS TRIP, said another. *All* of them were puppet shows.

Where had she put the one with no label? Cole looked around the room but saw no other tapes. Just more medical supplies, a bookshelf, a CD collection, a closet.

Maybe the tape was hidden in the closet. Cole walked away from the desk, heading for the opposite side of the room.

A flash of white shot out from under the bed.

A hand.

It grabbed Cole's ankle. He jerked backward and fell, hitting his head against the wall.

As Dr. Crowe rushed toward him, the hand let go and slipped back under the bed. Cole's breaths came in deep, panicked gulps. *Act against instinct*, he reminded himself. *Stay put.*

Dr. Crowe looked baffled. He hadn't seen the hand. But he knew what had happened. Cole was sure of that.

Kneeling on all fours, Cole peered under the bed.

There she was. Kyra looked out at him, ghostly and silent. Out of the darkness she slid forward a brown jewelry box. It was old and scratched, with a red stripe down the middle.

Cole took it and stood up. Now he had to find Kyra's dad. He gave Dr. Crowe a glance and the two walked out of the room and headed downstairs. The house was louder now. Lots more guests had arrived; they crowded the living room just about shoulder to shoulder.

Cole could see Mrs. Collins in the dining room. He recognized her from the painting on the wall, except she was a little older now. Her hair was all done up and she was wearing lots of makeup. Everyone was hugging her, handing her flowers and gifts and cards. Anyone trying to reach her would have a long wait.

Cole snaked among the people, looking for Kyra's dad.

A man was sitting alone in a small den, just off the living room. His back was to the crowd, and he stared off at nothing in particular, his expression dazed and his body absolutely still.

A few guests stood near him, just outside the entranceway, but they were all talking among themselves. They looked afraid of the man. No one seemed to be able to talk to him.

Cole elbowed his way past them and walked up to him. He looked like the portrait of Mr. Collins, but Cole couldn't be totally sure. The guy in the painting had a warm, smiling face. This man's face looked like stone. "Mister?"

The man didn't react.

"Excuse me, mister," Cole tried again.

Finally the man turned. His eyes were red and distant-looking, his face drawn and weary, as if he were slowly dying.

"Are you Kyra's daddy?" Cole asked.

At the mention of Kyra's name, the man's features seemed to fall inward. His eyes became glazed with tears and he nodded.

Cole's hands trembled as he held out the

jewelry box. "It's for you," he said. "She wanted to tell you something."

Mr. Collins stared at Cole for the longest time, confusion and grief playing across his face. Cole thought the two of them might stay locked in this position forever, but Mr. Collins finally reached out and took the box.

Gently he unhooked the latch and pulled open the lid.

Inside was an unlabeled videotape.

Mr. Collins took it out and turned it over curiously. Then he inserted it in his VCR, turned the TV on, and sat back down.

An image of Kyra's puppet stage filled the screen. Two finger puppets danced happily, speaking to each other in squeaky voices. Mr. Collins smiled, some of the pain lifting from his face.

Drawn by the sound, guests began crowding into the entry arch. Cole stood with Dr. Crowe.

On the screen, the puppet show abruptly stopped. The puppets disappeared, the stage was pushed aside — and all of a sudden, there was Kyra.

From the angle, Cole could tell the camcorder was sitting on Kyra's desk, directly across from her bed. Quickly, in full view of the camera, Kyra turned away and leaped under her covers. She flopped on her side and shut her eyes, pretending to be asleep.

The door opened. Mrs. Collins walked on-screen from the right side, dressed in a brown-and-orange-striped shirt and carrying a serving tray. On the tray was a glass of juice, a plate of fruit, and a bowl of soup. She didn't seem to know that the camera was running.

She checked Kyra, saw that she seemed to be sleeping, and said nothing. Then she walked quietly to the closet.

Cole couldn't tell what she was doing, but she returned holding a bottle. As she set it on the desk, the camera lens recorded the bottle's label.

It was floor-cleaning fluid. A skull-and-cross-bones poison symbol was visible near the bottom.

Mrs. Collins unscrewed the cap, turned it upside down, and poured some fluid into it. "That's too much," she muttered under her breath.

She dribbled a little back into the bottle, then dumped the rest in the soup.

Cole closed his eyes. He felt ill.

Around him the other guests stood open-mouthed.

On the screen, Mrs. Collins returned the bottle to the closet, then picked up the tray. She sidled around Kyra's bed and put the tray on a hospital-style rolling table.

"Kyra, time for lunch!" she called out, swinging the tabletop over the bed.

Kyra stretched and yawned, pretending to wake up. "I'm feeling much better now."

"I'm glad, honey," Mrs. Collins said with a smile. "Time for your food!"

"Can I go outside if I eat this?" Kyra asked.

"We'll see. You know how you get sick in the afternoons."

Kyra sat up and lifted the spoon. She took a sip, made a face, and looked at her mom.

"Don't say it tastes funny," Mrs. Collins scolded. "You know I don't like to hear that."

Kyra dipped the spoon back in the soup. With a tentative expression, she brought the spoon to her mouth and swallowed another gulp.

Mr. Collins lifted the remote with a hand that shook violently, and the screen suddenly went black.

He put his fingers to his forehead and stood up. His face had no more confusion now.

Only shock.

And betrayal.

And rage.

No one said a word as he staggered out of the room, but everyone followed. Every expression was a mirror of Mr. Collins's. Dr. Crowe looked furious. He and Cole fell in with the guests, following behind Kyra's dad like a loyal army.

Mr. Collins walked steadily into the dining room. There, his wife was rearranging one of the bouquets on the table.

He stopped in the entranceway, his friends close behind.

Mrs. Collins turned around and smiled tensely at her husband.

He did not smile back. "You were keeping her sick," he said in a voice hoarse with fury.

A tear rolled down his cheek and spilled onto the carpet.

Mrs. Collins looked from face to angry face. Her smile slowly went away.

The flowers dropped from her hands.

Cole's mission was done. He and Dr. Crowe quietly slipped outside and shut the door behind them.

Kyra's sister was completely alone now, still sitting motionlessly on the swing. Cole walked over and sat on the swing next to hers. He pulled the clown puppet from his pocket and held it out to her. "You liked it, she said."

The little girl just stared at it for a moment, then silently took it.

"Is Kyra coming back?" she asked.

It broke Cole's heart to have to tell her the truth. But he had to. Kyra was dead. And he realized now that he would never see her again, either.

"Not anymore," he answered.

CHAPTER 20

"Hold still, Cole," Mrs. Deems reprimanded. "If you're dressed as a poor boy, you have to look poor. It requires a great deal more stitches and safety pins to keep poverty in place!"

Cole loved the way she talked. So old-fashioned, like Bette Davis in those movies Mama liked to watch.

So much had happened in the weeks since Cole had been to Kyra's house. He wasn't afraid of the dead people anymore. He sent an anonymous message to Private Kinney's mother and Private Jenkins's wife. They were both still alive. He let the teenage boy show him his father's gun. And he gave him permission to throw it away.

The cabinet lady was the hardest. But she just needed to talk. No one had ever listened to her, she said. So Cole listened. She calmed down. She cried. And soon she went away.

They all went away. And they hadn't come back.

Dr. Crowe had been right. He was the best psychologist in the world. Cole felt so much happier these days. He was doing better in school. Kids weren't teasing him as much. In drama club, Mr. Cunningham said he had real acting talent. He and Mr. Cunningham were getting along now.

This afternoon was the big play, and Mrs. Deems needed to finish his costume. She worked deliberately, and she liked to talk. Twenty years ago, she said, she was having trouble mending a costume the day the backstage area caught fire. When the alarm went off, the boy who needed the costume was too embarrassed to go out in his underwear. He lingered a bit too long. He didn't survive.

And Mrs. Deems had never gotten over it.

It was a sad story, Cole thought, and he had

heard a lot of them. He stood still and listened while she mended the rip in his costume and strengthened the seams. "Now," she finally said, "move your arms around and stretch your legs. Let's see how I did."

Cole obeyed. "Feels pretty strong now."

"Lovely. Do you know your lines?"

"'Tell me, kind sir,'" Cole recited, "'of the reason for the boisterous clamor in yonder village green.'"

"Excellent!"

"How's my accent?"

Before Mrs. Deems could answer, the prop room door opened and Mr. Cunningham leaned in. "They're calling for the stable boy!"

Cole reached toward the table for his hat.

"Who were you talking to?" Mr. Cunningham asked, gazing around the room.

"Just practicing my lines," Cole said.

Mrs. Deems smiled sadly at Mr. Cunningham. "Dear Stanley," she said. "He was my favorite student. I suppose all his acting experience helped, didn't it? No more stutter."

Cole had avoided looking at her while she was behind him. Now he saw her turn away. The left side of her face, which had been burned off when she died in the fire, was no more than a big, bloody glob. As Mrs. Deems disappeared into the shadows, Cole faced Mr. Cunningham.

He hadn't seen a thing.

"Thanks for giving me this part, Mr. Cunningham," Cole said.

"You're welcome, Cole."

Mr. Cunningham was looking at him with fondness and confidence. Ever since he'd made peace with the dead people, he no longer walked around afraid. The other kids had sensed this, and had eased up a little. Cole found it easier to talk to them — and they were finding it easier to talk back.

No funny looks anymore. No "Eye." Mr. Cunningham didn't think Cole was a freak anymore.

Neither did Cole.

The two walked out of the dressing room and climbed the stairs to the stage. "You know," Mr. Cunningham said, "when I was in this school, there was a terrible fire in this section of the theater. They rebuilt the whole thing."

Cole nodded. "I know."

The rain slickened the streets and soaked Malcolm's overcoat as he ran to St. Anthony's.

He was late. The time had slipped away while he wasn't paying attention. That had been happening a lot lately. He hoped he could get to the auditorium before the curtain call at least.

He bounded up the stairs and into the building, then sneaked into the back of the darkened auditorium.

Young King Arthur was still in full swing.

Catching his breath, he glanced around for Lynn. Today she had her double shift, but she'd been hoping her boss at JCPenney would let her switch with someone else.

Malcolm couldn't find her, so he stood alone in the back, right in the center aisle. Fortunately no one seemed to notice his panting. Every eye was on the play.

The kids were posed stiffly on stage. Most of the boys were dressed as knights or gladiators, their chests made ridiculously bulbous by their plastic-armor breastplates, their heads dwarfed by helmets. Cole was standing in the back — *upstage*, Malcolm recalled from his summer stock days — and off to the right. *Stage left*, he thought. Or was it stage right? That was always confusing.

A boy in shiny fake armor strode to center stage, where the hilt of a sword jutted out from a large cardboard stone. The boy gripped the handle and pretended to pull on it with all his might. Sure wasn't Oscar material, but at least the kid succeeded in not budging the sword. Feigning exhaustion, he wiped his brow and slunk sheepishly back among the other "contestants."

Bobby O'Donnell, dressed in a magician's outfit, stepped forward. He was the chubbiest Merlin Malcolm had ever seen.

"Only he who is pure of heart," Bobby intoned, "can take the sword from the stone." The sword, of course, was Excalibur, awaiting the future King.

Bobby gazed dramatically around the stage at the boys playing the young village men, who all tried to act humiliated and scared. Bobby's eyes finally rested on Cole, and he said, "Let the boy try!"

The villagers all laughed and jeered, taunting Cole.

A boy in a hideous, ludicrously oversized villager costume limped forward. Malcolm had to look twice. It was Tommy Tammisimo, commercial star, hero of the third- and fourth-grade production not so long ago.

Tommy did not look happy with the casting.

"But he's the stable boy," he said in a dispirited monotone. "He cleans after the horses."

"Silence, village idiot!" Bobby bellowed.

Tommy limped away.

Malcolm was afraid that if he started laughing he wouldn't be able to stop.

Clearly Bobby enjoyed that line a lot.

"Let the boy step forward!" Bobby continued. With a grand gesture, he invited Cole to approach the stone. "Arthur . . ."

The stage fell silent. Cole took two steps toward the stone and suddenly hesitated.

Malcolm held his breath. Either Cole was a great actor, or he was terrified. Malcolm had seen that look on Cole's face before. It was the expression the boy had worn at their first meeting in the Sear house, when they'd played the mind-reading game. It said, *I'm nobody. I'm a freak.* It had been a part of Vincent Gray's expression in the bathroom, too, a shadowy remnant of the fear and confusion that had curdled over the years into rage.

I was picked first for kickball teams at recess, I hit a grand slam to win the game, and everyone lifted me up on their shoulders and carried me around, cheering. That had been Cole's fantasy once upon a time, at that now-distant meeting.

To him, back then, it was akin to his mother's dream of winning the lottery. An impossibility. A shot in the dark.

His Excalibur.

A psychologist found metaphors, relied on symbols. He had to, because the human mind did it all the time. Cole was only acting, it was only a play — but Malcolm knew. He knew Cole had emerged from his abyss awfully fast. Maybe too fast. He was bound to realize he could fall again — and if he did, he would fall hard.

But the look on Cole's face passed as quickly as it had appeared. He stepped forward and folded his fingers around the handle. A spotlight beam narrowed on him until the surrounding actors faded into shades of gray. And he pulled.

The sword began to slide out. The villagers let out a collective stage gasp. One by one they bowed low to Arthur the stable boy, their new king.

Light flooded the stage, and Cole suddenly seemed enormous. With a smile that radiated triumph to the back row, he held Excalibur aloft.

And then the kids were on their feet. They rushed toward Cole, whooping with joy. They swept him off his feet and held him high in the air, parading around the stage.

The parents in the audience stood, applauding and yelling bravo.

Cole seemed astonished. He broke into a giggle, trying to keep his balance. Below him, the eight-year-old arms began to buckle under the weight. Cole sagged, and then the whole mass of children slowly collapsed.

The kids were howling, all tangled in each other's arms and legs. Cole was shaking with laughter. Mr. Cunningham was propping himself up on the stage arch, his shoulders shaking.

And Malcolm was laughing, too, as he brushed away an errant tear.

CHAPTER 21

Cole brandished Excalibur above his head. Behind him, the rain pounded against the school lobby's stained-glass windows, projecting onto the floor amoebalike shapes that reminded Malcolm of a lava lamp.

Most of the parents and kids had left, except for those on the cleanup committee. Lynn had not yet shown up. According to Cole, her boss, Mr. Rattigan, wouldn't let her switch her shift so close to the peak holiday shopping season. But she had promised to pick up Cole after the play.

Thrust. Parry. Parry. Thrust-thrust.

Cole had seemed to take his mom's absence well, Malcolm thought. He was a strong kid. Not a bad fencer, either, for a knobby-kneed third grader. Next year, *The Pirates of Penzance*, perhaps.

For Cole, just about anything was possible now.

The case of Cole Sear was just about closed. Soon the boy would be on his own. It wouldn't be easy for him, ever. The ghosts would keep visiting, and he would have to work hard to help them. He had a gift, and gifts always carried a burden.

For Malcolm, the solution of Cole's problem was bittersweet, because it had come ten years too late to help Vincent Gray. But death, Malcolm now knew, was not what it appeared to be. Maybe because of Cole, Vincent would also be saved in a way — spared the need to walk the earth, like Kyra Collins and Private Kinney and Mrs. Deems and the cabinet lady.

Before he left Cole, Malcolm had one last item to settle. Something Cole had to do on his own, without Malcolm's help — the last loose end, possibly the hardest one of all. Cole had to come clean to his mom. She might freak out, but eventually she would understand. And her understanding was crucial to Cole's continued progress.

"How come we're so quiet?" Cole asked.

"I think we said about everything we needed to say," Malcolm replied. "Maybe it's time to say things to someone else? Someone close to you?"

"Maybe." Cole kept lunging with the sword. "I'm not going to see you anymore, am I?"

Malcolm knew what Cole's nervous energy was all about. Separation anxiety. He was feeling it himself.

Moving on was painful, but necessary. For both of them. Malcolm had his own family problem to solve.

He shook his head. It felt as if he were moving a thousand pounds. "You were great in the play, Cole."

Cole dropped his arms and turned to face Malcolm. "Really?"

"And you know what else?"

"What?"

"I thought Tommy Tammisimo sucked big time."

Cole gave him a grin. Malcolm tried hard to return it.

"You still look sad," Cole said.

Malcolm nodded. "I still haven't spoken to my wife."

"Why not?"

"I don't know. Never find the time. Whenever I get home, she's asleep."

"You can talk to her while she's sleeping. She won't know you're saying it, but she'll hear you." Cole began dragging his sword on the floor tiles, pacing nervously. "Maybe we can pretend we're going to see each other tomorrow? Just for pretend?"

"Okay, Cole." Malcolm exhaled very slowly and stood up. "I'm going to go now. I'll see you tomorrow."

He turned to leave, walking down the stairs toward the entrance, on the dancing globes of reflected raindrops.

"See you tomorrow," Cole said, his voice tiny and fragile.

Malcolm opened the door. He didn't dare turn back for fear of revealing his true emotions.

The pouring rain made it moot.

Lynn had been afraid Cole would be locked in the school by the time she arrived. But a group had remained to clean up, and after having kissed and congratulated her son, she and he had pitched in to help.

She heard what a great success the play was and saw Polaroid photos that had made her cry.

The Fazios had promised her a copy of their videotape, and their tough son Frankie had asked to play with Cole on the weekend.

Things had changed so much.

As she plowed home in the driving rain, her pride played tag-you're-it with her guilt. Neither won. The road was slick but her Volvo held the surface well, and they made good time — until they approached the city bridge. Traffic there was at a standstill both ways.

The old overpass was one lane either way, built for horses and buggies, like most of the city. An accident could tie up traffic for hours.

A few yards ahead, on the bridge itself, a car had jumped the sidewalk, smashing into the railing. Ambulances had squeezed between the lanes and flanked the accident scene, their red lights flooding the street.

Lynn tried to make out what was happening, but the rain would flood her windshield the instant the wipers swooshed past. "I hope nobody got hurt."

Cole didn't answer. He was sitting in the passenger seat, staring rigidly ahead.

"You're very quiet," Lynn said.

No reply.

He was upset. She knew it. She knew she

should have insisted more with Mr. Rattigan. Darren's mom was at the show, Tommy's mom and Bobby's mom. If she'd pushed a little harder, called a few more of the other workers maybe . . .

"You're mad I missed the play, aren't you?" she asked.

Cole shook his head.

"I have two jobs today — you know how important they are for us. I'd give anything to have been there."

Cole turned to face her directly. He had that odd intense look in his eye. That I-want-to-say-something look. The look that promised so much yet always ended up with a "Pass the Pop-Tarts" or "Can I sleep in your room?"

But this time Cole said something different. "I'm ready to communicate with you now."

"Communicate?"

"To tell you my secrets."

Lynn felt a sudden chill. She'd been waiting for this moment, but it scared her. Would she finally learn about the bruises and cuts? The violent writings and curses? The stolen figures from the church?

In a way, she'd hoped things would just work themselves out the way they had been doing over the last few weeks, without any dwelling in the past. Without explanation. "What is it?" she asked cautiously.

"You know that accident up there?"

"Yeah . . ."

"Someone got hurt."

"They did?"

"A lady. She died."

"Oh my God." Lynn wiped the inside of the windshield with her sleeve and tried to look up ahead. "You can see her?"

"Yes."

"Where is she?"

"Standing next to my window."

Lynn's heart thumped. She spun around toward Cole's window but saw nothing. "Cole . . . you're scaring me."

"They scare me, too, sometimes," Cole said.

"They?"

"Dead people."

"Dead people?"

"Ghosts."

No. This was not happening. She was not having this conversation with her son. But she couldn't *not* have it, either.

"You see ghosts, Cole?"

"They want me to do things for them."

"They . . . *talk* to you?"

Cole nodded.

"They tell you to do things?"

Cole nodded again.

Lynn tried to compose herself but she felt as if she were flying off in all directions. *He believes he sees ghosts. And he hides in a tent and has horrible murderous thoughts. What now? What?* Things weren't going to magically work out, after all. She'd been stupid to think they would. He'd need more help. But how could she possibly help him when she'd exhausted everything — when the loving home didn't work, and the school drama club didn't work, and the church and the psychologists and the parties and —

"What are you thinking, Mama?"

— And he was her son, the sweetest boy in the world, and she would die for him, *die for him* if she had to, if it meant she could deliver him to happiness from his dark fantasies. "I don't know . . ."

"You think I'm a freak?"

Lynn's eyes shot toward his. About this, she had no confusion. "Look at my face," she said levelly. "I would never think that about you — *ever.* Got it?"

"Got it," Cole replied.

"Just . . . let me think for a second."

Okay. All this stuff was real to him. Which meant — what? Deny it and upset him? Give in and risk that he'd never grow out of it?

"Grandma says hi."

Lynn's thoughts screeched to a halt.

"She says she's sorry for taking the bumble bee pendant," Cole continued. "She just likes it a lot."

Keep it together, Lynn commanded herself. *Above all, there is a reality. A real reality*. "Cole, that is very wrong. Grandma's gone. You know that," she said sternly.

"I know. She wanted me to tell you —"

"Cole, please stop!" This was crazy stuff. Cole was not crazy. Her son *was not crazy*!

"She wanted me to tell you, she saw you dance. She said when you were little, you and her had a fight, right before your dance recital. You thought she didn't come to see you dance. She *did*."

Lynn felt her hand rise to her mouth. How could he know that? She had no control now. She felt disengaged, floating, half-conscious.

The glare. The glare in the photos. He was different, wasn't he? He wasn't like other kids.

Cole's eyes were all she saw now. They were her mother's eyes, soft and sensitive but also stubborn, so stubborn. . . .

"She hid in the back, so you wouldn't see," Cole said. "She said you were like an angel. She said you came to her where they buried her. You asked her a question. She said the answer is, 'Every day.'"

Oh God. Oh God oh God oh God oh God.

"What did you ask her?" Cole whispered.

He knew. He knew things he couldn't have known. Things Lynn had kept only to herself.

She slowly took her hand from her face and told Cole the question she had never repeated to a soul. "Do I make her proud?"

The words released a decade of tears, the accumulated misunderstandings and unspoken sorrows of the two deepest relationships of her life.

Cole began to cry, too. Lynn opened her arms and he fell into them, crying and laughing and clinging to her as if to life itself.

She held him there, oblivious to traffic, feeling his little heart beat as relief washed over him like rain, holding tight to the son she would never doubt again, letting him know by her embrace that she had always been, and always would be, the mother he needed.

CHAPTER 22

Malcolm entered his house without a sound.

He had left Cole with a mission. Now he had his own.

The silence had to stop, the anger and secrecy. If it wasn't too late.

As Malcolm crept through the front hall, the harsh blue-white light of the television set emanated from the living room.

He paused in the doorway. Anna was asleep, curled up in a blanket on the sofa. Her skin was soft and translucent, her expression serene. Whatever she was dreaming had released her from the weight of sadness. When Malcolm was younger, he would watch her sleeping face for hours sometimes. He wanted the opportunity again.

The wedding video was running. On the screen, Malcolm and Anna cut their wedding cake, lifted two slices, and entwined their arms. As their guests roared approval, they fed each other and then kissed. Her expression that day was much like it was now. She was dreaming then, too. They both were.

Even after that day, they had not stopped dreaming. And they had not stopped feeding each other. Those had been the two cornerstones of their marriage.

Surely they still had some of the dream left. Malcolm wanted so to wake her, to watch the video together, to talk — but he didn't dare. She needed rest.

You can talk to her while she's sleeping, Cole had said. *She won't know you're saying it, but she'll hear you.*

Malcolm knelt next to the sofa, gazing self-consciously at the floor.

The truth. Only the truth.

"Anna," he whispered, "I've been so lost. I need my best friend."

"I miss you," Anna said.

Malcolm looked up in surprise. Anna's eyes

were still closed. She was speaking in her sleep, as if to someone in her dreams.

He hoped it was him.

"I miss you," he said.

She shifted slightly and spoke again in a voice thick and soft and very sad. "Why, Malcolm?"

"What, Anna? What did I do? What's made you so sad?"

"Why did you leave me?"

"I *didn't* leave you!"

Anna stopped moving, settling into a deep sleep again. Her arm slid out from under her head, her fingers draping themselves over the side of the sofa.

Something fell from her hand, making a sharp clatter on the floor.

It was a ring, now rolling in a slow circle, reflecting the lamplight.

As it came to rest on the parquet floor, Malcolm recognized it. Her wedding ring. He looked to her ring finger.

The ring was still there.

Malcolm was confused. If it wasn't hers, it had to be . . .

His wedding ring.

He held up his left hand. The ring was gone.

But he hadn't taken it off — or had he? Had he even looked in the last few days? Had Anna taken it, maybe — pulled it off while he was sleeping, some message that the marriage was over? That wasn't like her. And even if she had, even if her anger had made her act out of character, *why would she still be wearing her own ring?*

Nothing made sense. It scared him.

Something was dreadfully wrong.

He felt odd, weightless, out of place. He stood up and took a few steps back, glancing around the room. Everything looked the same but felt somehow different, as if the world had suddenly begun rotating the opposite direction.

Things he hadn't noticed suddenly jumped out at him. He saw the mail spilled on the front desk, unopened for what looked like weeks. Most were bills. The words PAST DUE had been stamped angrily on one. LAST CHANCE TO RENEW on another. IS THIS GOOD-BYE? on a third.

To the right, an old table had been jammed up against the basement door. Had it been there before?

The dining room table was set for only one place. But it was always set for two throughout the day. Always had been. No matter what had happened between them, he still had to eat. He still lived here.

Didn't he?

Malcolm felt as if a caul were being lifted from his face. The video ran on and on, Malcolm raising a glass, Malcolm toasting his wife — Malcolm but not Malcolm, an image of the past, of a young man who no longer existed.

A ghost.

Why was Anna watching? Why did a person fix on the past? To connect. To visit something lost, something left undone. That's what Anna was after.

That was also why Cole's ghosts visited him.

Shaking, Malcolm looked at his wife again. Her breaths formed little white puffs.

"No . . ."

Falling.

He was falling.

In his mind, he wasn't in the living room anymore. He was in the past, a year in the past, and he was falling, falling hard on his bed with a bullet in his side, and it was as if he were there again, seeing so clearly what he had since forgotten. There was another shot, in the bathroom, and Vincent was dead, that poor sensitive child had killed himself and it was Malcolm's fault, *Malcolm's fault*, and what was he going to tell Vincent's mother and —

Anna was screaming. She leaned over Malcolm now, pulling up his shirt

The bullet had made only a small entrance wound. "It's okay."

He turned onto his side and felt the blood coursing onto the bed behind him. He felt Anna's hands pressing against the exit wound, trying to stop the flow. *"Malcolm!"* she cried out.

"It doesn't even hurt anymore," Malcolm replied, groggily.

And it didn't. Because he was leaving already, separating, seeing it all at once, the bedroom, the shattered frame of the boy in the bathroom, and his wife clutching the body of her husband whose life's last pulse had just sunk thickly into the mattress —

"ANNA!"

His own cry shocked him out of the dream, and he was back in the living room and he knew now that it *was* all different.

They only see what they want to see.

Malcolm twisted himself to the left and pulled the back of his shirt forward. It was ripped open and covered with blood.

Where his lower back had once been was an ugly hole.

But he felt no physical pain. Only grief. For the life he had clung to that night and lost. For his wife.

For what had to happen next.

Anna was crying in her sleep now, and Malcolm knelt next to her. "Don't cry," he said.

She only cried harder, as if she'd heard him.

But Malcolm knew why he was here now, and what he had to say.

Cole's ghosts had appeared to him because they'd wanted something. Malcolm had taught the boy to give it to them. When they had it, they always went away.

Cole couldn't give Malcolm what he wanted. Instead, he'd done something better. He'd taught Malcolm how to get it.

What he wanted was simple. It was the hardest thing he'd ever had to do.

"I think I have to go," he whispered to Anna. "I just needed to do a couple of things. I needed to help someone. I think I did that. . . . And I needed to tell you something."

Anna shifted in her sleep. "Tell me," she murmured.

Say it, Malcolm told himself.

Just say it.

"You were never second," he said with all the conviction in his soul. "Ever."

Anna's falling tears were caught in the crease of a sad smile.

Malcolm was crying, too. "You sleep now, Anna," he said softly. "Everything will be different in the morning."

"Good night, Malcolm," Anna said.

"Good night, sweetheart."

As Malcolm leaned back, closing his eyes, Anna's breaths made slow, wispy clouds.

On the TV screen, the wedding reception was at its raucous peak. Malcolm was in the midst of his toast. Anna was behind the camera, keeping his face in full closeup.

"I just have to say," he announced to the guests, *"this day today has been one very special day. I wish we could all stay and play."*

The crowd laughed and Anna passed a joking comment that made the young groom blush.

"Anna," said Malcolm's image into the camera lens, *"I never thought I'd feel the things I'm feeling. I never thought I'd be able to stand up in front of my friends and family and tell them what's inside me. Today I can . . ."*

The tape was silent for a moment. Even the

shaky, grainy image couldn't hide the young groom's tears. *"Anna Crowe,"* he said with tenderness, *"I am in love. In love I am."*

The screen dissolved into static.

The room fell silent.

Anna Crowe slept soundly, her breaths invisible in the warm indoor air.

About The Author

Peter Lerangis is the author of *Watchers,* a popular, award-winning series of supernatural mystery-adventures for preteens. His new two-volume adventure, *Antarctica,* will be published by Scholastic in the fall of 2000. *The Yearbook* and *Driver's Dead,* his best-selling teen thrillers, have been translated into many languages, and his books for younger readers include *Spring Fever, It Came From the Cafeteria,* and *Attack of the Killer Potatoes.* Recent movie novelizations include *Sleepy Hollow* and *El Dorado: the City of Gold.* He lives in New York City with his wife, Tina deVaron, and their two sons.

ABOUT THE SCREENWRITER

M. Night Shyamalan [pronounced SHA-mah-lahn] began making films at the age of ten in his hometown of Philadelphia. At sixteen, he had completed this 45th short film. At age seventeen, he stood before his parents, both doctors, surrounded by pictures of the other twelve doctors in the family, and informed them that although he graduated cum laude and received academic scholarships to several prestigious medical programs, he had instead decided to attend the New York University Tisch School of the Arts to study filmmaking.

One evening, during his final year at NYU, Night sat down and began writing an emotional screenplay, entitled *Praying With Anger*. It was the very personal story of an exchange student from the U.S. who goes back to India and finds himself a stranger in his own homeland: In 1992, that became his first low-budget feature film. In July 1993, it was named Debut Film of the Year by the American Film Institute of Los Angeles.

In June 1995, he was asked to write the fantasy screen adaptation of *Stuart Little,* based on E.B. White's beloved children's classic.

In 1998, his second feature film, *Wide Awake,* was released. It starred Rosie O'Donnell. That film was shot entirely in and around the Philadelphia area and tells the story of the close relationship between a boy in Catholic school and his grandfather.

Next up is a new movie for Disney entitled *Unbreakable.*

Director's Cut:

Secrets of *The Sixth Sense* by M. Night Shyamalan

M. Night Shyamalan conceived of, wrote, and directed *The Sixth Sense*. To borrow a line from his movie, he's "ready to communicate with you" now and share his perspective on the movie, as well as unravel elements that continue to mystify.

Sometimes, you just get a picture in your head, and you get this feeling, "Wow, that would make a great story."

That's how *The Sixth Sense* began.

The concept for the movie came to me very early on. It was just this picture in my head of a child at a wake, after a funeral, sitting on the stairs of this house, and talking to someone who wasn't there. And I was thinking, How can I make a movie about this little child who sees the person who has passed on? For a long time, I didn't know quite how to do it, what the storyline was going to be. And then, I came up with the idea of a father–son relationship, which became, of course, the Cole–Malcolm story.

The picture in my head was one of the reasons I used a child, Cole, as the channel, the heart of *The Sixth Sense*. But it wasn't the only reason. Most of the movies I make have a child at the center, because they represent my point of view more accurately. Children have a sense of wonder and innocence, and a lack of cynicism, and most of all, the ability to believe. And so, in thinking about a story about ghosts, it seemed natural to place a child there.

Do you know why you're scared when you're alone?

There are aspects of Cole's character that are resonant of my own childhood. I was a very timid kid, very scared of being alone — almost phobic of being alone. My parents always had to arrange for someone to be with me. I hated being alone in a room. Of course, I outgrew that fear in my teenage years, but it was really salient and that is the feeling evoked in *The Sixth Sense*.

Malcolm's character changed a lot. He was originally a crime-scene photographer. Eventually that changed into a therapist. And that change came because I had to give the character a job that would naturally place him around the kid, without him having to call Cole up and say, "Hi, can you meet me at the ice cream parlor so we can talk?" Malcolm's profession had to be something where it would be natural for him and Cole to have set meetings all the time, a way for them to get intimate, without me — the writer — worrying about the practicalities of how this guy keeps coming to this boy.

Malcolm as child psychologist solved that practical problem. It also gave me a clear path to research. My wife is a child psychologist, and I sent questionnaires to all her teachers, and her colleagues. I asked lots of questions, including: "What would you do if a child said he saw ghosts?" "What would you do if a child didn't want to speak to you and he was being absolutely stone cold?" Also, "Would you ever cry in a session if a child told you something emotional?"

I got a lot of varied and interesting responses. I added them up and Malcolm's reactions were the collective result.

One thing about Malcolm that didn't change was his name. To me, a crow is sort of a bird of death. Crows give me an ominous feeling of hanging around, so that's what I named him. Besides, it would have been too weird to call him Malcolm Buzzard!

I see dead people . . .

I think it's in the realm of possibility that we can contact, or be contacted by, someone who has passed on. Certainly, I've met plenty of people who believe they are channels, but I don't have concrete evidence.

For people who do believe, it's generally agreed upon that there are spirits who have a difficult time passing from this current world — the state of the body — to some other entirely spiritual world. They have trouble leaving, so they kind of stay in an interim stage — in the image of what they were, and who they were. They have a hard time letting go of that. They're mostly in denial, they can't accept it. Those spirits don't even know they're dead. Often, they're the ones who have been wronged, and they can't leave until that wrong has been fixed. Or, like the little girl at the end of the movie [Kyra], they can't leave because they know someone else [Kyra's little sister] will be wronged. So they need to prevent [that] from happening before they can be at peace and move on. They need to have some kind of closure before they can leave.

While I have no concrete evidence of this, it makes sense. That's the way we move, right? If we're thinking of a million things in the morning, and we have a thousand things to do, we think we have a thousand days to do it, and then, all of a sudden, boom! That car accident happens in a split second. All that energy would have to go somewhere, it can't just vanish, I'd imagine.

My cousins and I always did the Ouija board — all the time. Only a couple of times did weird, weird things happen. One was pretty recent. We were in the basement of my uncle's house. The person asking the question did not put his hand on the board — the question was one that the rest of us could not have known the answer to. But the "ouija" answer came back so specifically, it freaked everybody out. 'Cause only the person doing the asking knew all the details. And he did not have his hand on the board.

If I *could* contact someone who has passed on, I might want to talk to [the legendary director] Alfred Hitchcock. I have a couple of questions for him!

But there is someone else. A friend of mine from college who died . . . not in a great way . . . I'd just want to make sure he was okay. I didn't try to bring my own feelings about this friend into *The Sixth Sense,* but a couple of times during the filmmaking, it did come into my head.

The questions that remain

The success of *The Sixth Sense* is very rewarding, especially that people are talking about it, dissecting it, going back to see it again, because that's how I make all my movies, to withstand that kind of scrutiny. It would be sad if you put that kind of minutia into it and nobody cared — it would be doubly painful!

Here are a few of the questions people still ask me.

**Did Cole know from the start that Malcolm was dead?*

The answer is yes.

Is that why, the moment Cole sees Malcolm, he runs to the church?

No, it's normal for Cole to sprint from his house to the church. He's not running because he's scared of the ghost.

Why isn't Cole scared of Malcolm?

The thing I found in the research, and that I generally find in kids, is they're very matter-of-fact about things. They're not like us. They're not so jaded that they go, "Oh, you're black, you're white . . ." Cole doesn't get scared of the person in the hall because he's a ghost, he's scared of the person in the hall because he's a stranger, and he's bloody. So to Cole, even though his sixth sense tells him this is a ghost, Malcolm is just a man, just this entity. So he accepts Malcolm easily — theirs becomes a normal relationship between man and child.

Are there other ghosts Cole hasn't been scared of?

Yes. It's insinuated that the priest who taught him Latin, and Cole's grandmother, among others, are ghosts he's interacted with, even had educational, beneficial, not scary relationships with. And the teacher who was burned in the fire at the school — the one who told Cole about "stuttering Stanley." Of course, Malcolm is the one that transforms him.

What's the deal with the red doorknob to the basement?

It's not just the doorknob. Anything that was tainted by the other world — the Sixth Sense world — anything that meant more than it actually was, was red. If you concentrated, you saw that the thing that was red — the coffee mug, Cole's sweater, Anna's dress at the restaurant, and of course, the doorknob — had some connection, some significance, some clue to the other world.

Is there some belief, some theory about that color?

No, I just made it up. It's a visual thing in filmmaking, the use of color to signify things.

If Cole knows that ghosts can't see each other, why does he expect Malcolm to see the hanging people at the school?

Cole understands that, but he doesn't understand every rule of everything. He doesn't necessarily expect Malcolm to see them, but he yearns for Malcolm to see what he sees. He goes, "You know, maybe you *can* see them, if you just are quiet."

None of his family and none of his friends can see them either, but in Cole's head, maybe he wouldn't be so isolated — a freak — if they could. If they were all really quiet and they did listen to what he was saying, they could get just the top layer, and they'd sense something, and Cole can go, "That's them." All Cole wants is for them to see just the peak of what he sees — which is the whole mountain. He knows that everybody can see just a little bit.

It's like teaching someone who can't see ghosts. You say, "Be really still. Do you feel something on the back of your neck? That's them. And that's as far as you're gonna see, but trust me, that's them."

How does Malcolm get down the basement when it's locked?

He's a ghost! He sees the door, tries to open it, thinks, "Why is this locked? Well, I'll go get my keys." He searches for the keys . . . and then blacks out. And the next thing he knows, he's in the basement. How'd he get there? He went through the door, as ghosts can. He can't acknowledge that, because then he'd have to accept who he is and what state he's in, which he's not ready to — until the end of the movie.

Cole says it gets cold when the ghosts are mad, but in the end, Anna's breath is cold, and there are no angry ghosts there.

Malcolm is there, and when he realizes he's dead, he gets very, very upset, and the room gets cold instantly. This spirit that hasn't been angry this whole time — the spirit of the man who lived in this house — suddenly realizes his life is over, and has been for two years! And all the emotions and anger, everything swirling, and he's just trying to hold onto it, but the whole temperature in the house starts to drop because he's very upset and angry.

I'm ready to communicate with you now.

When I was a kid I fell in love with [the movie] *Poltergeist* and others like that, so it made sense that when I grew up and made movies, there would be a whole generation of kids that would respond to it. That has been very gratifying. But what I most want people to take away from the experience of *The Sixth Sense* is hope — that maybe in the end there's some meaning to everything. That it's not so bad and that you *can* make sense of things. And to communicate. Because communication is a very important thing.

M. NIGHT SHYAMALAN